Footfalls

Short stories from

Scotland's west coast

HAMMERINN BOOKS

Published by Hammerinn Books

Ringing in Time Jane Wilkinson
Duggie Bob Toynton
Midges vs Mosquitoes Alison Dawson
The Road to Ruin Sylvia Smith
The Road Home Irena Chapman
The Path to Beyond Elspeth MacDonald
Tidal Strand Jeni Rankin
The Interview Elizabeth A Clark
A Feast from 'The Eyrie': Ben Lora Angela McDougall
Encounter – 13th February Alison Dawson
Hedgehog Highway Irena Chapman
Flotsam along the Underpath Alex Breck
Pony Paths Leonie Charlton
Writing 'The Path' Bob Toynton

Cover Photograph: Footpath on Raasay
by Julie Dawson

ISBN: 978-9999584-2-8

Contents

Snow Tracks. Photograph by Julie Dawson

Foreword

There are many writers in Oban and Lorn on the west coast of Scotland. Some of these writers come together on particular projects. This book is one such project.

We have called ourselves the Oban and Lorn Writers' Collective. There is no fixed membership, no actual organisation – just co-operation around a shared aim.

This book of short stories (and a couple of poems for good measure) explores pathways; whether in the landscape of western Scotland or through life. Often the two coincide. Sometimes they collide.

All profits due to the collective from the sale of this book will be donated to charity.

Ringing in Time

Jane Wilkinson

Rob took Jamena's hand as they started to climb the path through the bare silver birches. Matching their steps on the wide rutted track they gained height quickly. Sheep grazed the short grass amongst a few stunted trees. Jamena stopped to look back at the glen below and remembered another visit when Rob had taken her to Angus's Garden.

She turned and asked, "Can you see that bell we rang by the loch from here?"

"I think it's hidden behind the trees."

"Didn't you say it was a memorial garden?"

"Aye! For Angus Macdonald, it was created by his mother. He was a journalist murdered in Cyprus in 1957."

"It was so peaceful. We must have gone last May; I remember the azaleas and the rhododendrons were just beginning, a feast of colour and scent."

He smiled at her. "Not long after you first came to Oban."

They walked on and surprised a Blackface sheep. In its hurry to escape it tipped over the red tub it had been investigating. Rob walked over and righted the tub. He saw her questioning look.

"Sheep need food supplements in the winter."

The wind rushed at them as they rounded the next bend, making her bow her head in submission. She re-tied her scarf and pulled her hat lower. They laughed.

"The first blast is always the coldest. Look you can see the tops of the wind turbines behind that hill." He pointed up to the right. As she looked up she felt the bite of the next gust in her eyes.

Soon they could hear the regular swish of the turbines on the slope above them. They reached a large shed. Jamena could see a narrower path continuing beyond but Rob turned to walk up amongst the hill giants. Their size and beating hiss overwhelmed her. She had never been this close to a wind farm.

"I didn't know we had to walk between them," she murmured.

"Are you OK?" he asked.

"Hmmm! I just don't want to be around if one of those blades comes off; that one's crackling rather than purring."

He chuckled, "Come on, the Sheiling is close to the top of Beinn Ghlas and the view is worth a little suffering."

Jamena came to Argyll with a walking group from Sligo. Rob was first caught by the sight of her orange and green patterned head scarf before she turned round and he became lost in her sparkling dark eyes. He smiled at her, trying to ignore the sudden light fluttering in his stomach. Her answering smile was warm as he stepped forward to introduce himself to the group

"Hi, I'm Rob, your guide for the next few days; welcome to Argyll." Jamena did not hear much of what followed, just the deep timbre of his voice contrasting with his soft Scottish accent. Later, on the slopes of Ben Cruachan they fell into step.

"I've wanted to climb this mountain since we came on a family holiday to Oban when I was ten. It appeared in the background of nearly all our photographs."

"It's known locally as the Hollow Mountain," he informed her.

"Oh that's right I remember now, we went on a tour inside, it's a power station isn't it?"

"Aye, we'll be passing the dam and the loch on the way up. I'll point out the site of one of the main feeder pipes."

"Are you from round here?" she asked.

"My family farm locally, we have sheep and a few Highland cattle."

He went on to ask her about her life in Ireland and she told him about her father falling under the Irish spell when he studied dentistry at Trinity College Dublin, where she was now studying Irish Literature.

"But I thought your group comes from Sligo."

"We do, my dad applied for a post in a dental practice in Sligo when he returned to India to get married. My parents were betrothed at a young age. They moved to Sligo after they were married and have lived there ever since. Both my younger brothers and I were born there."

"Have you ever been to India?"

"No! But we are going to visit this September for a cousin's wedding. They want me to take my fiddle and play some Irish jigs and reels."

"That will be fun. Have you brought your fiddle with you?"

"I never travel without it."

"A group of musicians play Scottish traditional music in the Oban Inn tonight. If you felt like joining in I know you'd be made welcome. Perhaps your group would like to go there later."

She was invited to play with them that night and again on later visits to Oban. She stayed at the backpackers hostel and a strong friendship developed between her and Rob. Although her parents knew she went to Scotland with the walking group from Sligo in the holidays they had no idea how often she visited in term time, when based in Dublin. She hadn't told them about her developing relationship with Rob.

The whir of the wind turbines reflected her whirling thoughts as they climbed up towards the Sheiling. She knew she must talk to Rob about her parents' plans for her, but she was still reeling herself. How could they ask her to marry a man she had only met once? Did Rob see her in his future? She didn't want to force his hand. He would be shocked by the idea of an arranged marriage for her. She hadn't spoken to him about traditional Indian customs. She couldn't see a way forward.

His voice broke into her silence. He was pointing at two angular standing stones on the horizon. "We're nearly there. Look!"

She gasped as she took in the view. Loch Etive stretched out towards the green hills and beyond them dark mountain peaks. She walked towards the pair of tall moss-covered megaliths.

"They stand so close, one seems to lean towards the other," she whispered, as she stretched her hand out to touch the rough stone. Her eye followed the stone to its base where a pattern was etched into a slab of slate embedded at her feet. She bent down and followed the intricate motif with her finger, as a memory nudged her.

"Rob, these are similar to the ancient Celtic patterns decorating the Book of Leinster. My tutor took us to see it at Trinity College." Her class had been studying pre-Christian stories originally passed down orally before they were written up as "The Ulster Cycle", in the 12th century.

Rob took her over to one of the panels flanking the stones. The voice she had grown to love read the poem "Deidre of the Sorrows remembers a Scottish glen."

"Glen of the rowans with scarlet berries, with fruit fit for every flock of birds;

a slumberous paradise for the badgers in their quiet burrows with their young."

The seven stanzas spoke of the love Deirdre had for the landscape which now surrounded them, a potential paradise, one Jamena wanted to share with Rob. She had not heard the poem before but the story of Deidre and her lover Naoise from "The Ulster Cycle" was familiar. She had thought about it a lot in the last week. Deidre was beautiful and sought-after. King Conchobar of Ulster locked her in a tower with her nursemaid until she was old enough to become his queen. She avoided marrying him by fleeing to Scotland with her lover Naoise, and his two brothers. They settled by Loch Etive where they were happy for seven years. The King's spies found them and told the brothers they were pardoned and should travel back to Ireland to claim their lands. It was a trap. Naoise and his brothers were killed by Fergus of Ulster. Deidre committed suicide to evade having to be shared by the King and Fergus, her punishment for escaping to Scotland. She and Rob were here at a place that memorialised Deirdre's story. *"Arranged marriages,"* she thought and shuddered.

Having finished reading her the poem Rob smiled. "There have always been strong links between Ireland and Scotland. Sam Macdonald who commissioned this Sheiling married a girl from Ireland. They had often spoken of building something in the landscape to commemorate the links between Scotland and Ireland and tell the story of Deidre and Naoise. Unfortunately, his wife Evelyn never saw the Sheiling, as she died of cancer two years ago."

"Oh Rob, that's sad."

"Aye, but they had a happy life together."

He led her down the steps into the sheltered circle of the Sheiling. Warm coloured stones had been chosen for the retaining wall built into the hill and sloping down to an arc of boulders focusing the eye on the view. Rob showed Jamena a map showing locations of the place names associated with Deirdre in Glen Etive.

"My uncle owns a croft at Cadderlie. You can just see it over there on the other side of the loch."

She looked back at the key beside the map. "It says here that Deidre and Naoise probably lived there."

Jamena shivered. He put his arm round her and drew her back to the stone seat made in the shape of a Celtic knot. It was cold but he had brought a small rug and a flask of coffee.

She must tell him. Jamena knew the time had come. He handed her a cup and added a slug of whisky. She wasn't really listening to what he was saying.

"My uncle wants me to take on the croft and make it home. There is a small stone building which we could restore. Jamena, will you move to Scotland so we can be together when you've graduated?"

Had she missed something? Instead of responding to his question she muttered, "You haven't met my parents yet Rob."

Surprised at her response, he went on to reassure her, "I know, but there is plenty of time before the summer for me to come over to Sligo, I just need to know you want to move here?"

She could hardly speak. This was exactly what she wanted but it wasn't up to her anymore.

Rob blundered on, "I'm sorry, I thought that was what we both wanted, to be together."

"It is," she mumbled, "it's just not what my parents want."

"I don't understand, they haven't met me yet and it's your decision, not theirs."

"Oh Rob, I'm Indian, I thought my family were modern and this would never happen but there is an Indian friend of the family. I have only met him once, last year at the wedding." She stared ahead unseeing.

Rob got up to stand in front of her. His voice was quiet and controlled, trying to disguise his growing concern, "What are you saying Jamena? Is there someone else?"

"No! Not in my heart".

"Who is this man then?"

"He's a dentist coming to join dad at the dental surgery next month." She continued, the words tumbling out into the stunned silence. "Dad was made a partner last year and now the senior partner is leaving. My parents told me last week that they expect me to marry this man. He is helping with investment in the practice. I can't imagine life in Sligo with him. I don't know what to do. I am so frightened."

She was shaking and suddenly aware of the wind and the groaning of the turbines. Rob pulled her up towards him and she clung to him desperately.

"I am so sorry," she wept into his shoulder. "I'm scared, I love my family but it's my life. I can't marry a stranger for them. I love you."

He held her close and the wind stilled. He released her a little and cupped her face with his hands. Looking into her eyes his voice was loving and strong.

"I love you too, we'll face this together. I'll come back to Dublin with you tomorrow and we can visit your parents at the weekend."

She smiled at him gratefully but they both knew it would not be easy. Her parents would be hurt and upset. She felt torn between two cultures and the irreconcilable love for her family and Rob.

"I don't want to lose you or my parents Rob, but I will not give up my life to that man."

They looked out again at the view. The sun was shining on A'Chruach, known locally as Deidre's Sunny Bower.

"You can see A'Cruach from my uncle's croft, it's a sunny spot."

"Will you take me there soon?"

He returned her hopeful smile. "I'd like to do that but first we have to gain your parents blessing."

She sighed, glad she had told him, but not sure how they would navigate the strong cross currents of the coming months.

To lift her mood he gave her a quick hug. "Heh, maybe we could ask Sam if we could get married up here?"

They climbed back up the steps to leave the Sheiling. As she looked back at the view Rob rang the cast bronze bell hanging above them. It was inscribed in Hindi with a *pūjā*, which translates:

"I ring this bell indicating the invocation of divinity

So that virtuous and noble forces enter my home and heart

And the demonic and evil forces from within and without depart."

The Deirdre Sheiling. Photograph by Sam Mcdonald

Duggie

Bob Toynton

I only met Duggie once. I've never felt able to tell anyone about him, except some of the others in here. All we did was talk. I can still remember every word.

I was at that age when the duvet that is family stopped being cosy, safe and warm and started to grow heavy and suffocating.

It was the time before I had earned either the means or the trust to go off on my own but wanted nothing more desperately.

There was no fault with my parents. They were happy and earned enough to get by and to have a week or so's holiday each year. I dreamed of seeing those places I'd read so much about: the pyramids; the ruins of ancient Rome; temples on headlands above the bright blue waters and golden sands of Greece.

Every year we went to the same cottage in Argyll. It was as if to venture more than a hundred miles from home would break some invisible string and risk the three of us floating off like loosed kites. Oh how I wished!

The cottage was set below the crest of a spur in the mountains, not just at the end of a very long lane but at the ultimate reaches of the track beyond. The family car, only two or three years my junior, strained and heaved under the weight of supplies for the week. Our entertainment, as always, would be walking.

Progress on foot with my parents was always slow. They seemed to rejoice at every living thing they saw, whether flower, bird, insect or moss. As a young kid this had been great. I knew far more about nature than any of the others at school, as long as it could be found within a mile or so of that damned cottage. My parents' seemingly boundless knowledge did nothing to speed their progress or limit their disputes over this or that obscure leaf, twig or feather. I just wanted to see what was around the corners we never reached or over the hills we never climbed.

On the year I met Duggie I got my chance. My father had pulled a muscle heaving supplies across from the car, and a restful day loomed. Usually determined by heavy rain, I now dreaded having to fake enthusiasm for some old jigsaw with missing pieces. I had managed to squeeze the odd book into my meagre luggage ration, but I hungered to explore out there, in the wild, on my own, rather than in the pages of travels supplied by others.

I asked if I could go for a walk on my own and was hesitantly granted permission so long as I did not venture too far. In the weeks before the holiday I'd pored over the maps. The hill I had always longed to climb extended as a smooth slope for a further several hundred feet above the woodland that held the midges close to the cottage. What a view there should be from up there! But in the glen behind the hill, round the spur the cottage nestled below, was the real treasure: standing stones with ancient markings, or so said the map. I had never seen such things. Indiana Jones had had to start somewhere. This was to be my first few steps on the path to archaeological success and celebrity and all that would come in its wake. Maybe being fascinated by the deep, dead past was my adolescent, though bookish, act of rebellion against my nature-obsessed parents.

And so that morning I set off on my own. Now you have to remember that at that age we feel immortal and indestructible. It was a cool day right enough, but I would be going all that way uphill and didn't want the weight of a coat slowing me down. My parents made sure I wore my old boots but were assured that the hill-top was my only goal, and that recklessness was not in my nature.

Being on top of the hill was like flying for the first time. The views! And alone!

Then I descended on the other side of the hill, down into the small glen with only traces of little used paths – or were they sheep-tracks? As the map had suggested, there was no sign of habitation. Within the hour I had reached the first standing stone. I was in heaven, but not for long. I hadn't noticed the clouds gathering, and so the heavy downpour came as a surprise. Slipping off the wet stone by the stream resulted in me being both soaked to the skin and gaining a sprained ankle. Of course this was long before mobile phones, though I doubt if there would be a signal in that glen even now.

Packing a lunch for myself would have alerted my parents to my intention of being out all day, and the few biscuits I'd smuggled into my trouser pockets were now a mere thin stream-water porridge.

Nothing for it but to hobble on through the rain. It couldn't be more than a couple of miles down through the glen and then at some point, up and over the crest of the spur. But at what point? Nothing was familiar from this side of the hill.

That's when I met Duggie. At first I just heard something on the narrow path behind me. Then as it widened out, he walked along side me.

I asked him his name. I asked him if he was lost as well. I asked him where he had come from and where he was going. Then, just as I sat down exhausted on a large rock at the side of the path he said, "Duggie. They call me Duggie."

It could have been hunger or the cold soaking rain, but I think it was Duggie speaking to me that made me feel dizzy and struck me dumb for a minute or two. Eventually he added, "that's the name I've been given at least."

Duggie had sat down as well. He was just as wet and bedraggled as me. He looked up, putting his head to one side in a questioning way. Here he was, talking to me in perfect English, albeit with a west-coast accent. A dog!

At his urging I got back on my feet and continued walking. I could say we chatted, but he did most of the talking. It's funny how we all talk away to animals, but if they talk back we're stuck dumb. Two thoughts jostled for space in my head. Is this what hypothermia feels like, and if dogs understand English, what the hell must all those I've talked to in the past think of me?

Duggie chatted away, and I learned a lot. Had he not kept my attention I'm sure I would have just sat, or even lain down and fallen asleep. But on and on he went. Since he'd told me Duggie was his human-given name, I asked him what his real name was.

"Me," he replied.

So I asked him what other dogs called him.

"You .. or him, depending on the context."

At this, I just had to sit again. I insisted that everyone, everything needed a name, but he explained, in a frighteningly eloquent way, that identity is a very human thing. By nature a member of a pack, he needed no name nor identity. He just was. He did what dogs do. He interacted as positively as he could with other dogs and with humans, just like any of his kind would do. He was no different, so why would he need a name to single himself out, as humans seem compelled to do.

He also went on at some length about how he appreciated humans and especially his owner.

"Don't think we take all your kindness for granted; the food; the shelter; the love. It's wonderful to have a good owner, and before you say it, being owned isn't a bad thing. It's just part of being in a pack. To us it means belonging."

We set off, stopping to rest again several times. Each time I found it harder to get up and move on, but Duggie was insistent. It was as he finally started leading me up onto the spur, on what he seemed to know was the quickest route back to the cottage, that I sat down one final time. I asked him why, if dogs could both understand us and speak, there were no reports of this. "Can you imagine," said Duggie," how many humans would welcome a dog into their home if they thought we were listening in to everything they said or talking about everything they did. They'd put human motives on our actions. No! We're loved for our silence, our trust and affection, our inability, but in fact it is our unwillingness, to judge or comment. Food, shelter and love is all we want and all that should matter to dogs, and maybe to humans as well. Anyway," he continued, "we usually only talk when we know it will never be mentioned to anyone else." I must have shown my puzzlement. "When we know someone is about to die, we talk in order to thank them, but usually that's when we know they will never meet another human again. Right at the end of their life."

It was only at this moment that my own mortality hit me. "No," he added, "I think you might make it this time, but it was touch and go for a while back there." It was then we heard the shouts. "That'll be your parents out looking for you. They'll be here in a moment," and then he stretched his neck and lifted his muzzle towards the sky and in a very good imitation of my own voice, but much, much louder he howled, "Down here!"

The last thing he said was, "Don't speak to anyone about this, for your own sake, for your own future," and then he turned and quickly disappeared into the undergrowth.

I was found cold, wet and maybe even a little confused. That day I earned a good telling off for my foolishness and a deal of respect for having survived. I said nothing of Duggie.

All this time later and here I am. My parents are long gone. They always wondered what had got into me. Why my aims had so suddenly shifted. A degree in zoology later and then a successful career, but no fame, no celebrity, and finally this charity. My own family has come and gone. The kids had no kite-strings but just flew off to where they felt happiest. My wife has gone, and I may be following her soon. Still "Duggie's Rescue" is well established, managed by others now and funded well into the future. I still look after the dogs themselves, while I'm able. I'll carry on giving a home to those who are abandoned, neglected or maltreated, and I know now it will all continue long after I'm gone.

Every evening I walk around all the pens with their heated cushioned kennels and well-stocked food bowls. I always ask the dogs how they are and wish them a good night. I never use their names. I can tell they understand me. Now and again I catch in one of their faces the look that Duggie gave me as he left, and it warms my heart. One of these days I know they will sense something in the air, or maybe in my voice, and they will all talk to me. But that's fine now as well.

Ben Lora sunset. Photograph by Alison Dawson

Midges vs Mosquitoes

Alison Dawson

Hugh had been right. Carrying the tools from where he had left the quad bike had been hard work on such a warm day, but Dan had reached the muddy stretch of path and could see what needed to be done.

It had seemed fortuitous that the job interview tomorrow was taking place in Hugh's home town and Dan had taken the chance to catch up with his old mentor. Hugh had insisted on offering him a bed for the night and Dan had accepted, saying that he would like to spend the day on the hill before the meal in the hotel this evening, arranged to precede the formal interview tomorrow. Hugh had suggested that he could usefully spend the time on this path repair. A day of physical work outdoors seemed the perfect antidote to a long-haul flight and Dan had jumped at the chance. Hugh was retired now but had been Dan's first boss when he started as a path maintenance worker with the National Trust for Scotland during his university holidays. Having got his degree in environmental science, Dan had been employed full-time by the NTS and had worked his way up the career ladder to his present status as an environmental consultant, working at projects in various national parks in the UK. He travelled extensively and rarely had a chance to get his hands dirty these days. A laptop was his most vital tool now.

Dan had laughed when Hugh had started to tell him about the path repair and stopped him with a raised hand.

"You don't need to remind me of your mantra, Hugh. You drummed it into me often enough when I was a kid - *'Any hill path is only as good as its drainage'*."

Hugh had grinned ruefully. "Glad to know you haven't lost sight of the basics now that you're a top executive," he teased.

He was right, of course, and the widened slew of slippery mud in front of him was evidence of it. Dan set to with the pick and the shovel, glad that the breeze was keeping the midges at bay. The smell of the wild thyme brought back memories of his youth and reminded him why he had always loved his job. So why would he be considering a change of direction? He was well established with a good income and rosy prospects, so what was not to like? Was he perhaps in a pleasantly comfortable rut? Maybe the challenge of this job prospect was just what he needed. The approach had come out of the blue as he was enjoying a long anticipated holiday climbing in the foothills of the Himalayas. He had intended to spend the weekend with his parents on his return but had had to phone them from the airport to explain his change of plan. His father, always supportive, had said it sounded like a good opportunity. His mother, a past master of the meaningless cliché, assured him that 'what was for him would not go past him'.

His thoughts were interrupted by the high sound of children's voices coming up the path. He rested on his shovel as they approached. The woman leading the group introduced herself as the Head Teacher of the local primary school, explaining that this was a primary 6 and 7 outing to learn about the Countryside Code.

"And what have you learned so far?" queried Dan with a smile.

"To close gates," volunteered the bravest girl.

"Not to leave litter," offered another.

They were clustered round the adults, with a second woman bringing up the rear - younger with striking auburn hair. Presumably another teacher, or perhaps an auxiliary, thought Dan.

The terrified scream took them all by surprise. "Look, Miss. It's a snake! We'll all be poisoned!"

The children shrank back as one, a shrieking Mexican wave in reverse, apart from the biggest boy who had picked up a rock and advanced on the stone where the girl had pointed.

Dan leapt forward and caught his arm. "Stop! Don't do that. It's just a slow worm." He stooped to pick up the cause of the alarm and the Mexican wave reversed further but was thankfully silent now. "They are cold-blooded and they like to find a warm spot on a sunny day to sunbathe and warm themselves up. They're totally harmless. You do get adders in this sort of area sometimes but they have a very distinctive diamond pattern on their backs. You rarely see them because they hear you coming and disappear. Look, the heat of my hand is beginning to warm him and he is getting more active."

Indeed, the slow worm had raised its head and was coiling round Dan's wrist. As they watched he told them about the reptile's life cycle, what it ate, where it lived and the fact that it was technically a lizard rather than a snake.

"Is it slimy? Could I touch it?" asked one of the girls.

Dan bent down and the girl cautiously ran a finger along the worm's back. "Oh, come and try, Miss. It's dry and all silky. He's lovely."

Others crowded round and stroked the worm in turn till the teacher reminded them that it was picnic lunch time and the focus changed instantly. Off they surged up the path to find the picnic tables round the corner. The other woman didn't follow them and Dan looked at her quizzically. "Oh, I'm not with them," she explained. "I just followed them up by chance. I'm going to the top. It was good of you to explain to them about the slow worm. I'm sure they won't forget that."

"Well, at least they might pause before they batter the next one they meet," he smiled ruefully. "Conservation is largely teaching people about their environment and hoping they will learn to value it."

"I'm sure you're right. I'd better keep moving – I think the midges have found me."

Dan wiped the sweat off his brow and watched as she shouldered her backpack and started up the track. The wind had dropped and the midges – that curse of the Highlands – had taken advantage of it. He would certainly not miss them if he took the job in Africa. He supposed mosquitoes would be the problem there - a case of out of the frying pan into the fire?

The encounter with the schoolchildren served to highlight an aspect of his work which had begun to concern him. The main thrust of everything he had done over the years was to inform the public about the flora and fauna around them and to facilitate their access to it. What if the measure of his success was also the measure of the risk to which so many endangered species and fragile habitats were now exposed? As their advocate, was he also the instigator of their greatest threat? The thought did not sit well with him. For him the main attraction of the African post was that the whole ethos was diametrically opposed to that which had so far guided him. He would be working with impoverished communities which were currently destroying their environments for short term gain. He would be teaching them that instead of killing the gorillas for food and selling their babies to the pet trade, they could learn to protect them, construct the necessary infrastructure and build up a tourist trade which would bring jobs and sustainable income to the villages. A win-win result if it worked. It wouldn't happen overnight but in theory it was possible and the change of emphasis was appealing.

Later, walking to the hotel, he wondered who else was invited to the dinner. The letter from a Mr Crawford had simply said that *'it would be a chance to break the ice prior to the formal interview the next day'*.

"Dan Irvine? I'm Mr Crawford." The smiling middle-aged gentleman who met him at the door shook his hand. "Glad to meet you in person. Come and have a drink and let me introduce you to some of the others. We're just waiting for a couple more before we go in."

The group at the bar turned at their approach and Dan thought he recognised a couple of familiar faces from conferences he had attended but knew he would struggle to remember the names. "Ah, here she is now," said Mr Crawford. "The last member of our interview panel - Hazel."

Dan turned, his hand outstretched, to face his auburn-haired encounter of earlier. His smile froze. "We've already met," he said to Mr Crawford. "but she didn't introduce herself. In fact, you could say she has already interviewed me in a covert sort of way. Quite sneaky really."

He was furious and felt he had been taken advantage of.

"Yes, we've met," confirmed the woman, "but I didn't recognise you."

"As one of the interview panel you will have received my cv with photo attached," countered Dan.

"Sure," said Hazel, "but the photo was of a short back and sides clean-shaven businessman in collar and tie which bore little resemblance to the bearded Neanderthal in mud-splattered shorts and a sweaty t-shirt I met on the hill this morning!"

She turned to Mr Crawford who was now wringing his hands in consternation at this development, two red spots on her cheeks betraying her annoyance.

"If Mr Irvine feels he has been hard done by perhaps I should step down from the interview panel. I can always submit a written report on my impressions of my meeting with him earlier if it would help. I would not care to be complicit in any unfair procedure."

"Oh dear, surely that won't be necessary." Mr Crawford turned to Dan beseechingly. "Hazel works on the project in Africa and I've sat you next to each other at the table to give you a chance to get to know each other better. Perhaps I should go and change the table placings." He looked as if he was on the verge of a heart attack.

"No, that won't be necessary on my account," said Dan. "If I can cope with twenty hysterical primary school children, I'm sure I can handle a redhead with attitude!"

The green eyes flashed but she didn't rise to the jibe and Dan felt ashamed. "I'm sorry, that was below the belt. I think I'm overreacting. I'm just back from a month climbing in the wilds of Nepal and facilities for personal grooming were not much in evidence. Please accept my apology and allow me to escort you in to dinner."

Was there the tiniest hesitation? But she took the proffered arm and they proceeded into the dining room where he pulled out her chair and seated her before taking the chair on her left. Mr Crawford's breathing resumed its normal pattern.

"Thank you," she said, "every inch the gentleman. And it's auburn, not red." He couldn't decide whether she was teasing him or being sarcastic.

Whatever else this African job would be, he had a feeling it would never be boring.

Stock image

The Road to Ruin

Sylvia Smith

It was a different kind of Friday night. Lorna had been allowed to invite several classmates to her home to get ready for the end of term school disco. Her mother had prepared a big pot of spaghetti Bolognese and a heap of garlic bread. As they giggled and gossiped their way throughout the meal, the girls ate only token amounts.

Marion resigned herself to scraping the plates, placing them in the dishwasher, while muttering under her breath. "What a waste!"

Marion Gilchrist, thin and nervous, had not allowed her daughter much freedom recently. Calum, Lorna's twin brother, had been lucky to escape injury, when the car in which he was travelling back from a shinty tournament in Mid Argyll, had gone off the road.

She rued the day she had fallen for the dubious charms of Sandy Gilchrist. He was a typical, self-styled, West Coast hard man. A dinosaur, who's like was hopefully heading for extinction. When she had worked as a catering assistant on the ferries that linked the islands to the mainland, Sandy had been one of her best customers as he travelled backwards and forwards to jobs in the Inner Hebrides: hard worker, heavy drinker, piper, Gaelic singer, chancer who could talk his way out of almost anything.

Only two weeks ago, at a fundraising ceilidh for the pipe band, the jovial *fir-an-tigh* looked round the audience, seeking out someone to humiliate, to raise a laugh. "I see we've got Marion Gilchrist here tonight. Sandy Gilchrist came home sober the other night. Until then, Marion didn't know he took a drink."

The audience guffawed. Marion blushed but did not smile. It would have been funny, had it not been closer to the truth than anyone could imagine.

Determined to give her children a clear understanding of the dangers of alcohol, she insisted that they watch a documentary together, where the presenter, a doctor, in a humorous and self-deprecating style, explained that, as alcohol creeps insidiously into the corners of your brain, it takes the body back through the pathways along which you have progressed since birth.

There were clips of him and his co-presenter in various stages of closely monitored intoxication. With his healthy good looks and his well-toned body, they had laughed and called him Doctor Flash.

In the marshmallow pink bedroom, a slowly deflating birthday balloon emblazoned with the number sixteen, wobbled in the draughts of their transformation from school pupils to fashion icons. They left the house in a mist of mixed fragrances.

Mrs. Gilchrist called out, somewhat desperately, to her daughter. "Remember Doctor Flash!"

"Yes, Mother!"

Her friends shrugged their shoulders at this mysterious message. Lorna rolled her eyes heavenwards, applying a bored look to her face. She boldly made a V sign towards the closing door, as a symbol of her integration into the pack.

Inwardly, she recalled the pact she had made with her mother about the upcoming night out.

1) Home by midnight

2) Stay with your friends

3) No alcohol

The hall was disappointingly half empty when they arrived. They shuffled together on the floor for a bit. Lady Gaga, Rihanna, all the usual suspects vibrated from the speakers. Tina, one of her friends, was a year older than the rest. Illness had kept her back a year at school, but she fitted well into the group. She was destined to be a leader, whatever direction her life would take.

Tina's large sequined shoulder bag sparkled spectacularly with the disco lights. She lifted it from the floor and beckoned to the girls to follow her to the cloakroom. In a quiet corner she took out a tube of Pringles. "I'm not hungry" declared Lorna.

Tina peeled back the silver foil and deftly tipped the tube up. She slid out a slim bottle of Morgan's Spiced Rum. "Let's get stuck into this!"

As they slugged from the bottle Lorna at first refused, remembering the television presenter, with his gleaming white teeth, his crisply laundered shirt, open at the neck, his trendy trainers and his immaculately faded jeans.

*

Without alcohol, we are rational beings, capable of decision making, of keeping ourselves safe.

*

When the bottle came round the second time, encouraged by her pals' low chant of "Drink! Drink! Drink!" she succumbed. "One can't hurt." she supposed.

*

Often, the decision to drink is made as a result of peer pressure.

*

The liquid heated her mouth and burned slowly down to her stomach. It was a new feeling. She did not hesitate when the bottle came round again.

Just then, the caretaker poked her head round the door, spray bottle and mop in hand, taking an opportunity to check on any high jinks in her dominion, remembering that in her day it had been a half bottle in the handbag. "I hope youse girls are behavin' yerselves!"

The newly empty bottle was swiftly replaced in the cardboard tube and pushed down to the bottom of a rubbish bin.

As they returned to the dance floor Lorna's heart was racing. Her cheeks were pink. As a warm glow spread through her body, she linked arms with her friends, swaying rhythmically to the loud music that blasted her ears. *'This is the best night of my life!'* she thought.

*

When a small amount of alcohol enters our brain, we feel relaxed and affable.
Everyone is our friend.

As the night progressed Lorna discovered that Tina was not the only one to covertly convey illicit alcohol to the disco. After she had sipped from a shared water bottle, already laced with vodka, she trembled a little as the strobe lights wrapped themselves round her body like snakes. She leaned in close to her friends, telling them she loved them as their faces grew from pinheads to giant balloons and shrunk back again.

*

Further into the journey away from sobriety, we become the stroppy teenager, questioning rules and finding reasons to ignore them.

*

Tina beckoned to the group who followed her outside the hall, where they cooried conspiratorially behind the big industrial bins, as a cola bottle, perfumery and sweet, already infused with Bacardi, was shared into paper cups. When empty, the cups became missiles. She found it easy to swallow vodka soaked Gummy bears that sloshed around the bottom of a small plastic food container, in a brightly coloured alcoholic soup.

*

If we continue to drink, we lose control of our body's reflexes, wobbling about like a toddler, trying to find its feet.

*

Her head spun. She staggered as she rushed in the direction of the toilet. Her friends followed, now looking scornfully at the cubicle door as she loudly emptied the contents of her stomach.

*

When our body feels in danger of being poisoned by over-indulgence in alcohol, it tries to protect itself. We may vomit.

*

"Silly wee bitch, thinking she could keep up with us."

They propped each other up as they sashayed once again into the foyer.

*

At this point in the journey, we may become self-centred and argumentative. Think of the toddler and the terrible twos.

*

Only Tina remained. "C'mon pet, let's get you out into the fresh air."

Tina steered her towards the exit. Lorna cried pitifully, wiping her streaked make up and her snotters on her friend's silky shoulder. A strong gust of wind whipped in from the bay, combing flat the floral displays in the ornamental gardens that surrounded the hall. The cold air hit her like a steel cricket bat. Together, the pair reached a low wall. They slumped recklessly down on the grey concrete.

"We will have to wait here for the others."

"Why?" wailed Lorna. "I need to go to sleep."

"Oh no, you mustn't sleep. We need to get you home. Please Lorna, talk to me."

Lorna leaned in to her friend and began to snore. Tina began to worry.

*

We may feel we need to sleep, regardless of the safety of our situation.

*

As the sound of music from the hall faded to silence, the remainder of the group of friends clattered down the steps and joined the pair on the wall. Lorna woke, unsure of where she was.

*

We will be disorientated.

*

"You two still here?" The tone was now unfriendly. This pair had let the side down. They couldn't hold their drink. "We thought you would be tucked up in your cots by now."

The group began to argue about which of their parents should be phoned to do a *"taxi"* run home.

"I can't go home", wailed Lorna "My old dear will kill me!"

*

Our mood can be unpredictable.

*

Unexpectedly, Tina slapped the trembling girl on the face. "Shut the fuck up! You're more trouble than you are worth."

*

At this stage of the journey, we are completely disinhibited; we may even become violent.

*

Lorna and Tina began to push one another. Tina heard a loud crack as they slithered off the concrete ledge. As Lorna lay on the ground unconscious, blood flowed from a deep cut at the back of her head. One of the girls saw the large white van, with its bi-lingual markings, cruising slowly down the street. "Aw no! It's the polis! Get up! Hurry up! Try to look sober."

Tina remained kneeling by Lorna. The others took off along the track at the back of the building.

*

We may become unconscious, incapable of standing, of communicating, of controlling our bodily functions. At this point we are completely dependent on others for our personal safety. We have reached the stage of the new born infant

*

Meanwhile, in the Gilchrist house, the red numbers on the bedroom clock showed 23.59. Marion, who had lain like a coiled spring, watching the seconds charge towards the agreed homecoming time, tumbled herself out of the bed. Lorna usually kept to her promises.

This was no Cinderella moment. She began to get dressed. She was intent on going out to search for her precious daughter. She had barely pulled up the zip on her jeans when the phone rang. "Hello! Is that Mrs. Gilchrist?"

Marion's whole body shook violently as she held the phone near her face. The voice sounded official. "Yes, speaking!"

"This is the Accident and Emergency department of the General Hospital. We have your daughter here. She has been in a wee incident."

Charging out of the house like a woman possessed, Marion jumped into the car and drove through the darkened streets with total disregard for the Highway Code.

In the Accident and Emergency area of the hospital, on a chair outside the treatment rooms, sat Tina, wrapped in a blanket of misery. She looked down at her feet. "I'm really sorry, Mrs Gilchrist. I should have looked after her better."

The anxious mother shook her head. She slid in behind the blue pleated curtain to see her errant daughter; her head was bandaged, her face was streaked with rainbow colours of makeup, while clear fluid steadily dripped its way down a tube into the cannula in her hand.

Lorna painfully raised her head. "Shit! It's my Mum."

"Well, who else would it be?"

"Please don't say *I told you so!*" pleaded the girl.

Some weeks later, the young offender sat between her parents, outside the room where members of the Children's Panel met. Sandy Gilchrist, self-employed, was losing a day's work and a day's earnings to attend this meeting. He muttered in a low breath, "All this fuss about a few drams!"

Marion stared numbly at the gap between the posters on the wall. Silence was her weapon as well as her armour. Sandy's summons to appear in the Sheriff Court on Tuesday was positioned threateningly behind the clock on the mantelpiece: refusing to provide a urine sample, driving under the influence of alcohol, dangerous driving, and police assault. There was no way he would wriggle his way out of this one. Almost killing himself and his son didn't even come into it.

For Marion, this was the end of the road.

The Road Home

Irena Chapman

And now, leaving the city behind,
the motorways, wider roads,
all the trappings of faster travel . . .
my heart lifts.
Don't worry about the camper vans,
caravans,
boat and sheep trailers.
Allow yourself time.
Allow yourself to breathe.
Allow yourself to see.

And yes, slower traffic is frustrating once you
know the road,
the twists and turns, safe places to pass,
familiar landmarks that mark your progress . . .
but remember.
Remember how you, new to travelling
these roads,
new to this place, were
lifted by anticipation,
lifted by expectation,
lifted by the landscape.

And as valleys open out to vistas of hills,
as mountains and water beckon in the distance
and snow poles welcome like a guard of honour,
light . . . shifts.
Shadows chase each other across the hills,
ripples dance on lochs and rivers,
and trees: sheltering, screening, colouring,
shaping.
Welcome to this world.
Welcome to this life.
Welcome home.

The Path to Beyond

Elspeth MacDonald

There's a petrol station by the turn off and I stop and buy some horrid cheese there. I know it will be horrid before I eat it but it's the best food in the shop. The shop has typical petrol station fare. Racks of chocolate bars in wire baskets flank the front of the counter and there are rows of drink and fags behind. The cigarettes are chastenedly hidden in black drawers. I wonder how Iain knows which drawer to go to. He smiles as he accepts the money for the plastic cheese. Rumour has it that he loves money, smiles when he accepts in – cries when he has to part with it. I don't know. He always seems nice to me. He's old. So old that his ears have started to sprout bushy white fronds from the leathery skin. Game though, for an old fella, chased two burglars one night, threw his torch at them, jumped in his car and pursued their van. The Police advised him to stop, said they'd get them. But they didn't. Iain just had to suffer the loss. I resist the urge for the two-for-one sweeties that a star of day-glo cardboard is advertising and go out down the step back to my bike, shoving the cheese in my pocket.

I feel right under the mountain here. It rises straight up out of the ground over the road, drawing your eyes up to the miniscule sheep stuck to its side of scree interspersed with green. There is a pick-up on the forecourt. Dogs bark from within and a man with dirty boots is taking out a load of petrol cans, laying them next to the pump. He's from beyond, I'm sure, some way up the road anyway. I don't look at him, but it increases my excitement and my awareness that this ordinary petrol station is a portal.

I cross the road and take the turn off. At first, it's like any other side road that meanders along a river. Pretty but not wild. People with shiny cars and manicured gardens are living here. Big windows serve as widescreen televisions into countryside they won't venture into. They probably don't have the shoes for it. Fuck your shoes, take them off! I'm too excited, I know. Manic. I've got to watch myself. I could live here forever though, never go back. I cycle up the tarred road, swooping from side to side. The rhododendrons and azaleas from people's gardens smell amazing and I'm intoxicated. I cycle up the hill, standing up on the pedals and feeling the burning in my calves. I fix my eyes on a tree, if you can get up to that, I tell myself, you can get off and push. The bike leans with my weight, slanting the view from left, to right, to left, to right. I cycle past my tree. I tricked myself. I always do. I'll fix my gears one day. Back downhill. Exhale, freewheel. I pass the turnoff to the big house and remember working there. Big sandstone castle. We had to replace the chimney with concrete blocks. You could pull the sandstone apart with your hands. I said to the Laird: "You know your castle is made of sand" and he laughed. He was all right, knocking down a wall in the garden with a mash hammer. I offered him the big persuader from the van, but he wouldn't borrow it. I start to climb now, forestry road, recent extraction has covered the ground with bark, soft feathery sheaves floor the hardcore. I'm looking down on the loch, bright blue, deep and icy looking, plunging down from the steep wooded slope. A radio is blaring out from somewhere down by the kelp-slippery rocks: probably a fish farm worker, there's a fish cage there, a big black circle sitting just out from the yellow lichened stone. The path drops violently downhill and the bike frame rattles, my entire body vibrating, I look down at my brown forearms locked into place on the handlebars. They're a blur of juddering. I laugh aloud, inhaling dust and insects. Above me the contrary road is climbing again and way, way up I can see it clinging to the edge of a cliff where at some point the rock had to be chiselled away to make way for it. I breathe in the whole scene, inhaling the solitude. I feel the world recede and know that this is where I belong, on the road, on this road particularly, because, it transports you back in time. Down this road it is the same as it was when I was born, earthy smells, beech tree trunks velvet green, tufts of grass in the middle of the road, parts of it have been the same for centuries. When I get to where the river flows into the loch, a sandy fan of an estuary flowing into the glittering sea, when I see the Bailey bridge that even the first time I saw, I somehow remembered it, I feel a resonance. It fits. But I will cycle on past. Past the house with the apple tree and on up the track though the glen because I will always want to go further. I should have been a nomad, a Gypsy, a drover, a tramp, I don't belong anywhere, but this is the closest to belonging anywhere I have ever been. I am free here, a refugee from the world. I head up the glen as peewits tumble down from the blue, nearly hit the yellow spangled ground and soar back aloft with reedy cries. This is the past in the present and it is real, and I am more alive here than I am anywhere else. I can cycle all the way up to Black Mount and not see a soul. I want to run away here. If I get a terminal disease, I will spend the last of my days here. I've promised myself that, or is that another lie? Why do I have to be dying to allow myself to live? My own garden at home is a narrow slice of land, polytunnel, three hens, flowers and polite green grass. I've got neighbours on either side. Tarmac, hot tubs. I'm the only one in the street with a front garden, didn't turn it over to car parking. A tiny sliver of the world where no wildness is allowed. Even the path behind the house must have its verges strimmed by an army of volunteers in hi-vis vests. What are they volunteering for? To rid the villages of night scented stock. To chop up the slow-worms? Nature must be controlled, flowers must be in tubs, grass must be short, cars must be cleaned. Fuck off. The Extinction Rebellion calls but crowds and shouting are not for me. I was not built for any of this. I dream of peace, starlit skies, swimming in lochs and drinking from burns. I dream of a path out.

A North Uist beach. Photograph by Bob Toynton

Tidal Strand

Jeni Rankin

Douglas slapped his folded gloves repeatedly into his hand and shouted at the groom, "Come on Thomas, when's this going to be ready?"

Thomas fumbled threading the reins with fingers made clumsy by Mr McDougall's dark mood. "Nearly finished sir" he said, buckling the last leather strap with relief. The horse Rusty turned his head towards him with a seemingly baleful stare, as if he'd seen it all before.

Douglas stepped quickly up on the carriage and took the reins. "Tell Cook I'll be back for dinner" he said, then clicking his tongue and twitching the reins, he encouraged Rusty over the sloping grass to the beach. He glanced back at the house, fancying he saw a movement in the bedroom and, for a brief second, thought it was Eleanor, until he realised it couldn't be. The pain struck him deep as he remembered he'd never see her again.

Rusty knew the tidal path across the Vallay strand well and picked his way carefully. As Douglas listened to the rhythmic suck and pull of his hooves on the wet sand, he found his mind going back to when they'd first met. He'd been in London staying with his friend Sidney and had been invited to a small soirée. After the musical entertainment, they'd been mingling with the guests and it was her laughter that first caught his attention.

He looked across the room to see a pretty young woman of medium height with auburn hair, standing with a small group. Someone had said something that amused her and she was laughing, not loudly, but wholeheartedly. She said something back to the others and they all joined in the merriment.

Douglas turned to Sidney: "Do you know that girl over there with the auburn hair?"

Sydney glanced at his friend smiling and looked across. "You're in luck," he said "that's Eleanor Graham. She's a lovely girl, very popular. I'll take you over and introduce you if you like."

He laid his hand on Sydney's arm, "Let's be a bit more subtle than that. Do you know any other girls in the group?"

"Well, yes, I do."

"So, let's wander over in a minute to talk to them and introduce me to them all."

Sydney smiled, he knew his friend didn't share his bold approach to women. He strolled over and struck up a conversation with the three girls he knew and then introduced his friend. He was slightly surprised to see Douglas talking to two of the other girls before he spoke to Eleanor, but he did move closer to her as he spoke. Sydney decided to wade in. "It's going to be a lovely day tomorrow, why don't we all meet up for a stroll in St James's Park?" A couple of the girls said they weren't free to come but Eleanor said she would be delighted and Douglas caught Sydney's eye.

The next day, Sydney had rounded up some of his friends to join them and they made a jolly group. He glanced back after a few minutes and saw Douglas and Eleanor had fallen behind the others.

"This is such a beautiful park" said Douglas "I do enjoy coming here when I'm down."

"Why are you in London?"

"I have some business to do."

"That's a Scottish accent isn't it?" ventured Eleanor. "Where do you live?"

"Well, until recently, I lived on the mainland, but I've just had a house built on an island."

"An island! You live on an island?"

"Yes, on North Uist in the Hebrides."

Eleanor stopped walking and turned towards him, and he noticed how green her eyes were. "I have no idea where that is," she admitted, "tell me about it."

He was more than happy to do this and told her of the beauty of the place: the clear seas, white shell sand beaches, heather uplands and coastal machair. She smiled as he painted his word pictures for her. They both lost track of time and eventually realised they'd caught up with the others at the end of the walk.

Looking back across the park, Douglas said, "I'd forgotten there were ducks here. I should have brought some bread with me."

"We could have fed them," said Eleanor. "maybe we could do it tomorrow?"

"All of us?" he asked.

"Why not just us two?" Eleanor replied.

They met up the next day and took another stroll round the park. This time stopping to crumble bread between their fingers to feed the ducks, laughing as they waddled and squabbled at their feet.

Afterwards Douglas suggested they have tea and he took her to the Grosvenor Hotel in

Victoria. Over the hot, clear tea and sweet cakes, Eleanor was charmed by Douglas's gentle nature. He was not pushy like other men who had shown an interest in her, he seemed perfectly happy to move at a slow pace which suited her.

"What made you decide to build your house on Uist?"

"Well, I've always spent a lot of time in the islands and finally decided I'd like to live there permanently. They're unique in their beauty and peace."

"How often do you come down to London?"

"Well, not often, but as and when I have to." He told her of his business manufacturing linen and how much he'd expanded production since taking over from his father.

Eleanor poured him another cup of tea as she listened. She liked the way his eyes lit with enthusiasm when he talked of his beloved Scotland; it all sounded so delightful. Douglas was a few years older than her with the first few flecks of grey in his brown hair and beard. She liked the way he listened attentively, his brown eyes looking into hers, when she spoke about herself. Picking up on her love of art, he suggested they go to the National Gallery the very next day and see some of her favourite paintings.

Douglas was beginning to worry that he should be starting the arduous rail and coach journey back north, but decided to delay a few more days. Eleanor's captivating company was a good excuse to defer his return.

The day after their trip to the National Gallery he took her to dinner at the Langham Hotel in Marylebone. He told her a tale of what local people on the island got up to and it amused her and he realised how much he loved hearing her laugh. He was even more pleased that his story had been the cause. Eleanor asked him to tell her more about Scotland and he warmed to his subject again, talking of the sea crossings, the run of the tides, the changing weather and the beauty of the scenery.

"I've never had my feet off dry land" laughed Eleanor.

"Well you can't get to the islands without getting aboard a boat or two."

"I've never been as far afield as Scotland and you make it all sound so enticing."

He looked at her across the table, he longed to reach forward and hold her hand but lacked the courage. He wondered if he should ask his question then but, suddenly unsure, he looked away. "It's almost…." he hesitated, "magical."

At the end of the evening, as he delivered Eleanor to her parents' home by hansom cab, she asked if he would join her tomorrow at a tea her mother was having. It took him a moment to agree and note the time he was expected.

There were quite a few people there but Eleanor sat next to him and they soon dropped into their easy conversation whilst sampling the tiny sandwiches, scones and fancy cakes. Her mother made a point of talking to Douglas, her curiosity piqued by Eleanor spending so much time with him.

The next day he invited Eleanor to dinner at the Savoy, hoping the palatial surroundings would lend him courage. After their main course he reached forward and took her hand. She looked slightly surprised but didn't withdraw it. "Eleanor, we've not known each other long but I know how I feel about you. Would you do me the honour of becoming my wife and coming to Scotland with me?"

Eleanor smiled broadly "Yes Douglas, I'd be delighted."

He released a breath he didn't realise he was holding and impulsively kissed her hand. "Why thank you my dear. I must speak to your father tomorrow before we chose a ring."

Douglas was relieved her parents had no objections apart from his living in Scotland. Her mother said, "But you'll be so far away dear, we'll never see you."

"But Douglas comes down on business every now and then," Eleanor turned and touched his arm as she spoke, "and I can come with him."

It was the first time she'd reached to touch him and he felt thrilled by it. He put his hand over hers. "I come down on a regular basis Mrs Graham, and you'll see Eleanor then."

Her mother and father soon realised that neither Douglas nor particularly Eleanor would accept any doubts about their plans.

It was quickly agreed they would marry in London and honeymoon in Scotland. Eleanor was almost as excited about the romantic sounding journey up to Scotland as she was about marrying Douglas.

He'd already spoken to her about the train routes to Edinburgh and how they could stay in the striking new railway hotels on the way. With careful planning, they could get almost to the coast by train to take a boat out to Uist.

It was all settled in a remarkably short time, but then Douglas was used to organizing complicated issues. Eleanor's family, although disappointed they didn't have time to have a big society wedding, could not deny the happiness that shone from Eleanor's face.

Before the couple knew it, they found themselves in the station, the smell of hot oil and burning coal wafted over them as their train wheezed and huffed at the platform. Waving goodbye as their cases and boxes were loaded on, they finally settled into the carriage and Eleanor snuggled up to Douglas, the first time they'd really been alone together. He put his arm around her and bent his head to kiss her for only the second time, the first having been at the end of the marriage service.

During the journeys over the next few days, Eleanor plagued him with questions about where they were, what town was this and whose castle was that? He delighted in introducing her to the landscape, towns, cities and the architecture.

As they left the bustle of Edinburgh and travelled west, Eleanor commented on the lack of towns and villages along the way. She was entranced as they neared the Highland mountain ranges and gasped at the beauty of the route to Fort William. The last part of their journey was by horse and carriage until they left the mainland for the islands. Eleanor did not travel well over water and was relieved when they finally made landfall again on Uist. She stood on the pier at Lochmaddy with her cases and boxes around her and realised, for the first time, she was truly in the middle of nowhere. And it was cold and they still hadn't reached home.

Thomas was there with the carriage and they were soon bumping along the track to Sollas when she finally saw the house Douglas had described so vividly. Standing a short way off the coast was the island of Vallay and the magnificent house stood proud on the horizon. They had to wait for the tide to recede to uncover the strand path, then Thomas edged the carriage forward until Rusty found his rhythm and picked his way over the sandy ground with a pace learned from constant repetition. She noticed a small bluff covered in grass on the way to the island and then they were there. The staff were all out to greet them and it seemed to her lights shone from every window. The house enfolded them in its warmth and she was relieved to find it was delightfully cosy.

The house had the latest design of central heating, and fresh water was piped over from the main island. Generators provided electric power backed up by candles, and there was always good peat available for the fires if required. Within the house you had everything you could need.

Instructions had been sent ahead and the servants had prepared two bedrooms, one facing seaward and one towards Uist. He showed them to Eleanor and asked her which one she would prefer as her room; she immediately chose the one facing Sollas.

Initially she was occupied in getting to know her husband's ways better, and settling into married life. Intrigued by his interest in archaeology, they kitted her out with a pair of good boots and dresses more suitable for exploring the landscape. She went with him to the standing circle at Pobull Fhinn, the burial cairn at Barpa Langan, the wheelhouse and the ruined broch. He showed her the places on Vallay where he had been exploring ancient sites to rediscover the past. The fine dresses she brought with her were rarely needed here. There wasn't much polite society in which to socialise.

One day he took her to a sheltered white sand beach. First helping her down over the shallow rocks then standing with his arm round her shoulder. "This is my favourite beach. Sometimes I come down here to watch the sunset."

Eleanor laughed. "But you can see the sunset from the house."

"Yes, but it feels closer here facing the endless sea."

"It seems so empty."

"What does?"

"The sea, so wide and deep."

"In the summer, I come down and bathe here. The water's a bit cold but I love it."

Eleanor laughed again, "You must be mad! You wouldn't catch me going in the water."

"But it's not that deep here, the beach slopes gently quite a long way out."

"I'd be too frightened to go in."

He pulled her closer and kissed her on the forehead. "Then you shan't have to my dear."

Douglas was unfailingly kind and any little thing she desired he would order and have shipped up for her; she wanted for nothing. Except it was not enough; somehow, she was fading. For the heart's dreams are sometimes false and the rainbow's colours can fade. She no longer laughed as readily as she had, the light in her green eyes was paling. She often sat at a window and stared across the water to Sollas. She never looked seaward.

As summer's light dulled to the short, dark days of winter, she became wary of the weather driven seas that lashed their shores. The winds would howl round the heights of the house like unquiet spirits, leaving her unable to settle to a book or her sewing. Douglas would draw the heavy curtains to conceal the storms, putting more peat on the fire which emitted its distinctive sweet smell. He would often play the piano for her or encourage her to join him on the stool to play a duet.

Their life was constricted by the tides and, in deepest winter, the weather. Douglas seemed to know by instinct the relentless rhythms of the seas but still ensured there was a list of tidal times in the kitchen for all to check.

Eleanor was relieved as the winter softened to spring and she felt able to venture out more, occasionally wandering the island and speaking to the tenant farmers who laboured there; often going with Douglas when he crossed the tidal strand to Uist and into Lochmaddy.

Sometimes when the tide receded, she would have a picnic packed and encourage her husband to join her on the island bluff half way across the strand where they would sit in the sun and eat and drink wine. They would chat as easily as they ever did and fall into their affectionate ways. But, somehow, it did not seem enough. Something was withering within her and Douglas's heart ached to find out what it was and put it right. If he had any business off the islands, he would always encourage her to accompany him so she could enjoy some society in the towns and cities on the mainland.

He planned a trip back to London and Eleanor agreed so rapidly to accompany him, he became afraid she might not return to their island world. He felt she did not thrive there as readily as he did. His roots were deep, delving back to the prehistory of the place, he was all too aware hers hardly seemed to have caught at all.

They stayed with her family in London and, for a while, she became her old self, the laughing Eleanor he'd fallen in love with. She took him to see her friends and relatives and ensured he also spent time with his own friends. Despite his fears, she showed no reluctance to return to their island home, although she did not have the same sparkling enthusiasm as on that first journey north. He could almost see her spirit withering as they drew closer.

On their return he spent the night in her room, lying with her after their lovemaking, holding her close. When she woke, he had gone, but must have returned to place the rose that lay on her pillow. She held it up to smell the scent and felt its soft petals on her cheek as a tear brimmed.

Over the coming weeks Eleanor took to rising early and walking along the shores, sometimes even braving the shell beach where Douglas had been surprised to find her footprints. If the rain did not drive her home earlier, she would always return for breakfast.

He would never forget the summer morning when she had not come back. Everyone turned out to search. It was some time before they found her, at the white beach, facing seaward. She was floating on the incoming tide. Calling out her name, he plunged in to catch hold of her turning her over and seeing her lifeless face. He howled with pain.

Douglas felt as if his heart had been wrenched from his body. His lovely, laughing Eleanor was gone, never to return. Over the coming weeks he wrestled with wild imaginings that his beloved island had somehow killed her. That she had withered and died away from her natural habitat and the waters had claimed her.

Unable to cope with her loss, he was sunk most evenings in drink. Sometimes he did this at home, but he felt her absence more deeply in the house. More frequently, he would cross to Sollas, sitting in the local tavern drinking himself into painless oblivion. Others watched the tides for him, ensuring he was safely packed back on his cart with Rusty leading his sure-footed way home. The servants would help him off the cart and Thomas would brush and stable Rusty.

Except this last night. After he left Thomas impatiently that morning saying he'd be back for dinner, he didn't arrive. The servants became concerned as the tide started to rise but, knowing how the tidal times chimed with him, concluded he'd decided to take board in Sollas. It was morning before they discovered the truth.

He had set off late from the tavern leaving only just enough time to beat the tide's flow. Rusty had started at his usual steady pace until he was nearly half way. Douglas, having taken more drink than he thought, fell off the cart and lay insensible on the damp sand. The horse bent down and nuzzled at him, but he was out cold. The tide was fast advancing and Rusty whinnied and worried at him but to no avail. As the waters crept up past his fetlocks he backed away. Now neighing in distress, he stumbled with the cart to Sollas, but all were abed and no one heard his distraught calls. In the morning they found him standing with the cart, his head bowed low. They immediately clambered into boats and set off but found they were too late. The same coastal waters that took Eleanor had also claimed Douglas.

The Interview

Elizabeth A Clark

Idly she looked at the scenery, it reminded her of Argyll and the digs she was cartographer on. She snorted at that word – she was just good at technical drawing and noting distances, elevation and bearings on paper. It was the trees she was motoring past that brought the memories to the surface; she thought of that last dig, in a beautiful wooded glen with water slithering through the bog into the burn on its way to the not so distant sea, and Iain. A sudden change in tyre sound alerted her to a changing road surface forcing her mind away from memories best left alone.

A turn, a blind bend the road deteriorating into a farm track, the deciduous trees were just leafing, the pale greens gentle and fresh. The land was waking from its hibernation. Her thoughts refocused on the current 'assignment'.

Yet she still could not let the past go, the poem 'The Road Not Taken' by Robert Frost kept playing on a loop – now annoying her, she had to concentrate; her pathway had been laid that fateful last day of the dig, and Frost had it right.

Still her memories flowed in, at first just vague flutters of impressions – meeting the other 'slaves' (volunteers), the professor and his clique, above all that the smells of the dig – earth, water, grass, compacted ancient earth, the noise and smell, griddling the earth and the growing spoil heap. One face superimposing itself on the dig – Iain… coffee, their first meeting – over an iced-caramel coffee no less. Alexandra smiled, he'd managed to walk straight into her, the sticky mess going all over her, leaving both of them laughing, her sticky, damp and feeling a few years old again!

Iain, he had rather shamefacedly admitted his name, turned out to be a thorough gentleman. Helping her grab anything that could absorb the dripping edifice that was – no! She shook herself forcefully, best not to think about how he'd kitted her out in (for her) overly large jog-pants and top – his; he'd provided his waterproof laundry bag for her very, disgustingly sticky, clothes.

Cracking her window slightly she caught the scented pines and rowans, the lower scents of grass, water; heard the cry of buzzards invisible in the sun, heard the finches in breast-bursting song, the gulls hanging in the air currents flaring wings scanning the loch. Her driver's mirror view morphed into Loch Nant, Loch Eil, Loch Etive – God she hadn't thought about these three digs in years, her memories still too raw for processing.

Odd, she missed Loch Eil the most, in spite of her heart-breaking memories.

The external sounds captured her awareness, taking her right back to Glen Nant and its side glen, the road snaking alongside the loch, of parking alongside student bangers, lecturers and volunteers almost new, safe, cars. The walk to the site, setting up – her priority was the 'mapping table' – paper, pencils and location.

But, always, Iain in the background, always there no matter what. Rounding a corner on auto-pilot she was blinded by the sun – she was back, physically it seemed, back on site, holding the board, drawing, the wood scent was so strong it hurt. Then she heard the chain saws, her muscles twitched in phantom movement of sharpening her pencil, the slightly rubber smell to remind her of the rubber resting between pinkie and ring finger. Then another turn on automatic and her memories burst away as she began to consciously plan her approaches, then she saw her destination.

What is hope? What is unease? What is charity? Alexandra MacLeod wondered as she continued up the uneven track and towards a darkly forbidding house, incongruously set in bright sunshine (for now) and meadow land. All other thoughts flew out of her mind as the door was flung open as she drove up to it.

A mental checklist sped through her synapses – cold logic, fear, trepidation, caution. Call it journalists' precautions or her highland lineage coming to the fore (she knew which she preferred). For the first time Alex left the car keys in the ignition and surreptitiously fielded her work keys... Just. In. Case. She thought. Just. In. Case.

How much to tell him, how much not to tell him and – should she 'fight dirty'? She thought as she watched him stalk towards her. Yet hope still gave her the impetus to exit the car in a professional manner... hmmm. She had often heard the phrase 'he had/has gimlet eyes' and often wondered at it, now no more. Alexandra was worried, just what did the commentators mean, or are they prescient, somehow she didn't believe that. She caught the smell of danger, or thought she did.

Usually she ended up confused which is a situation she hates, just ask her friends and work colleagues, this time though...this time – wow they were spot on with this 'guy'. In fact, it took all her 'professionalism' to continue to straighten up and wait for him to come nearer before speaking. "Hi, I'm –"

"I know who you are". Wow, aggression personified she thought.

"No I don't think you do, I'm from the Times here to interview a Mr –"

"So? What do you want to 'interview' me about?"

There was an animalistic quality to his movements, build, face and speech, frightening in itself, yet also compelling in a sick sort way. Alexandra really wished herself many miles away, safe with friends and, yup, her colleagues; go figure she thought. I really wish him far, far away from me NOW.

The more he talked – a gruff, grating drone, the more she incrementally inched backwards towards the car and safety.

They both jumped as her mobile tone pierced the air, her shaky hand flips the phone open, eyes registering the callers ID. Oh thank goodness. "Sorry I have to take this, if you'll excuse me?"

Alexandra quickly gets in her car, surreptitiously pressing central locking, sighing mentally, already composing a broadside to 'the Ed', instead, she answered the phone with: "Jake, you so bloody owe me." She could feel him wince as his tinny voice echoed in her ear.

"Er, yeah, about that – are you safe? You're not with him?"

Alex started rooting about in her bag, producing pad and pen – have to look as if it's more instructions for the interview she thought as she asked, "Jake, what aren't you telling me?" Forcing a smile for 'the hulk' prowling around the car. "Jake?"

"Are you in your car? If so, lock the doors, start the car as if for heat, and get the hell out of there."

"Jake?"

Silence, then another voice came over the ether, a voice from her past – a voice, no, accent she trusted. "Just take it slow lass, if you can drive away safely nod and do so. Trust me, please, just do it." The line went dead. Shit! If they could see her it meant that there were either binoculars or a 'scope sighted on the situation, probably both. *Oh Jake what have you got me into?* She thought.

Alex had never told Jake, but if unsure about the situation and she was in the car, not only were the doors locked, windows up, but the engine was idling, it was just a matter of going into first – easily done as she could be adjusting the heating, and could then take off. Now it was just a question of hand brake off and steering initially with only her non-dominant hand whilst pretending to have a conversation with a 'dead phone' before dropping it in her lap.

Thank goodness the car had passed its MOT only two days ago was all she could think as the wee car metaphorically hoisted its skirts and took off like the proverbial bat out of hell, no screech of tyres, flying gravel, no smoke either, just nought to sixty, in first, in ten seconds flat!

Alexandra concentrated on the road, her forward vision – her steering, until she rounded the second bend where she had to perform an emergency stop, or else plough through a road block comprising three police cars and two trucks. She promptly let the car stall, she was safe, she was free...

White-knuckle grip, not seeing, faint, Alexandra let her head rest on her cramping hands beginning to shake-shiver, white noise irritating and blanking out everything.

"...She's in shock," the voice faded in and out of hearing, wavering as it continued "get a medic up here... I don't care... I have a casualty in shock... get him up here, now... Lass, can you open your door please?"

Huh? Oh, right... he's speaking to me isn't he? Alexandra thinks.

"Lassie, open your eyes... look at me... you are safe." That annoyingly trusty accent and voice again. She frowns, trying to remember something about that particular voice and person it was attached to. She hears a scuffling sound and flinches away; and again that gentle voice.

"Lassie, it's okay, Jake's given me your spare key... I'm opening the car door (a gust of wind tainted with exhaust fumes, forest – and a pleasant aftershave indicated that, Alexandra thought) ...Now then, I'm going to release your seatbelt – sorry I'm going to have to stretch over you (a gentle presence, a slight weight, then a click and her body was released) ...There now, can you give me your hands?"

Alex just continued shuddering.

"Okay, lass my hands will help you release the wheel – on three (she could hear an impishness in his voice, *I am sooo going to find out who this 'voice' is* mused Alexandra). One. Two. Three" and a warm hand enclosed her frozen right one, he gently moved his fingers around, eventually capturing the nearest hand, lifting it off the wheel.

"Shall we do the other one? But you just let me put this on for you," and she felt a mitt going over her right hand, which he then placed in her lap. "Right, your left hand lass, do you think you could release your death grip? The mitt I've got for it is lovely and warm."

Tentatively Alexandra's muscles relaxed enough that her fingers twitched, a warm hand gently helped and then – wonders – warmth from the mitt spread over her cramped hand as he worked it on.

"Hey lass, that's good. Can you move your legs out for me? Good girl (this, as Alexandra complied as much as she could, his warm hands once again helping cramped, panicked muscles) ...okay I'm just going to wrap this around you (warmth once again, body recognising a fleece, whilst brain accepted that she was being wrapped in an emergency blanket of some kind) ...Now can I help you stand?" A nod. "Again, on three – One. Two. And three, hup!"

He gently guided Alexandra away from the roadblock, arm around her back, supporting her, the other arm used as a bar – that she was gripping, hard, very hard. Then his voice, soothing and comforting came into her left ear. "That's it lass, soon you can open your eyes. All's well."

Strangely for Alexandra, she relaxed, her head nodded down to his shoulder and she felt herself slipping away.

She came to, groggy and strapped to a gurney. "Hey, get me out... I hate being confined… come on, please." Alexandra tried to scream it aloud.

Then she hears 'the voice' and tries to turn towards it, pulling against the restraints, fear on her face. "Hey there," a gentle hand touching her wrist, "how you doing?"

She tries to talk, he must see the panic in her features, as he grips her forearm kindly yet firmly, distracting her, making her focus on something else.

"Hey no problem, don't worry…I'm going with you to A and E, so I'll be able to fill you in on what's been happening, and I'll keep the piranhas away." He must have been watching Alexandra intently as he whispers, "It's all right to sleep now."

The man watches as a small smile lights up her face – she got the reference to the needle wielding nurses and the rest of the press…

Alexandra doesn't even hear the ambulance doors close or the engine cough into life, even the gizmos she's attached to are barely heard – but are understood to be there. She slips into unconsciousness, unaware that her questing hand has found and is gripping 'the voice's' hand.

Her mind replays a loop of memory – the people on the dig that year, the blazing arguments between the dig director Dirk and Iain about his commitment to the dig – or was it mountain rescue? Her confused mind jumbled the events and faces, the time and locations, the other rows, always started by Dirk, the power he abused in firing volunteer diggers and support 'staff'; his bullying of the students and PhD students, the surety that Iain had that Dirk was creaming off some of the finds.

A bump, rock and her back screamed agony at her, confusing her even more - why couldn't she remember, all that flitted through her mind were shreds of Robert Frost's poem "The Road Not Taken". With lucidity failing her she determined she would tread the road less travelled, especially if it led to the path back to … She faded into oblivion.

Iain, held her hand, silently praying she'd be okay, he'd given up trying to find her after their 'adolescent' argument so long ago, he needed the new path finding her again gave him. Now was the time for a change and a joint pathway – as it should have been if he hadn't been so stubborn a lifetime ago.

Ardmucknish Bay from Beinn Lora.
Photograph by Robert Hamilton

A Feast from 'The Eyrie': Ben Lora

Angela McDougall

Reeling from the feeling of vertigo,
kids now nested on the blanket,
we're pecking at the picnic, perched
and teetering on the brink
of a real life OS map, far, far, far beneath,

on this high, over Connel, we point out the airport
noticeable as small straight lines above the caravans;
fanning parallels echoing the bridge
across the Etive and the edges of the sea,
geometric cuttings on a charted scene.

With daring glimpses, directly down
we catch seagulls as they soar
in a gorge of lurid trees,
vibrant in their circling cries,
and all this,

topped with fields and loch, then
houses and hills, and a final lush squoosh
of cloud swirled sky, stacked like pancakes
filled full with the scent of spring,
delicious in this surprising presentation,

makes us want to fly like Icarus, but land,
way down there, on a small straight line.

Encounter – 13th February

Alison Dawson

She was going to run out of time. Reaching the top of the pass she looked back at the winding path and realised that the sun was setting in the west. In contrast to the full-blown extravagance of a summer sunset the mid-February version was shaded from the palest blue through mauve to delicate shell pink and was heart-stoppingly beautiful. The foot of the empty glen was already lost in the gloom of the coming night. It wasn't until now that she remembered that 13th February was the anniversary of the Glencoe Massacre. For a moment she thought of the night centuries ago when this path would have witnessed the desperate plight of the fleeing MacDonalds seeking refuge with their kinsmen on the Appin peninsula. Today's peaceful vista would have been awash with pain and terror as the clansmen fled for their lives from the treacherous Campbells. Historical accounts speak of a blizzard that night. The Campbells had set upon them as they lay sleeping and those who could had fled with no time to prepare. The chief had been killed as he scrambled into his trousers. His son, returning from a meeting in Inveraray, had arrived to find most of the homes in flames and his clan either dead or missing. History relates that he spent many days combing the hills searching for the scattered survivors and helping them to safety. The dark and the snow had allowed those who knew the terrain to make good their escape, but it was no night to be without shelter. Young and old, women and children, many barefoot and poorly clad, were ill-equipped to cope with such harsh conditions. There had been many burials in the following days.

The climb had been tougher than she expected and had taken longer, meaning that now she had a problem. She could go back the way she had come to her parked car, but it would certainly be dark before she reached the bottom and the path was narrow and steep. The alternative was to carry on, circling the hill until she hit the hill road round the shoulder which would take her down to the roadside more safely with an easy walk along the main road to her car. Although she knew the hill road well, she did not know the middle section of her planned route. The track, designed to give access to the hill for stalkers and their vehicles, did not go further than the col. From there on she had been given to understand that the path was less used and harder to follow. Shrugging the backpack onto her shoulders she resolutely turned east and strode on hoping to hit the hill road before the light finally went.

Just lately it had felt that the myriad calls on her time had multiplied. Her mother-in-law's clinic appointments, various rotas for the children's activities, helping her husband with the business paperwork, the everyday cycle of household chores - it had all seemed to mount up. Normally she relished the challenge of keeping all the balls in the air but lately she had begun to crave some 'me' time. For her that had always been hill walking. Ill-advised though it seemed she had seized the chance of this free day when it presented itself.

The path soon petered out but it was too late to turn back. Cursing her stupidity in thinking she could accomplish this walk in the short winter's day she pressed on, finally admitting defeat when she tripped and rolled down a scree slope. Accepting that she faced a night on the hill she fished in her pack for her torch, survival blanket, flask and chocolate. *'Well'*, she thought, *'you've got your 'me' time now – a whole freezing night's worth of it!'* At least she had done one sensible thing and packed her back-up essentials. They were in fact minimal and assembled in haste to allow her to tick the 'sensible and well-prepared' box rather than a realistic assessment of what she would need in just these circumstances. For a start, she had no spare battery for her torch. Her family, knowing her plan, would soon be expecting her. She checked her mobile, knowing as she did so that there would be no signal here. How long before they hit the panic button and subjected her to the mortification of the mountain rescue team?

The wind had risen bringing with it intermittent flurries of sleet. It would be a long night. She hunkered down behind a bolder for shelter turning up her collar and drawing the thin survival blanket round her. In spite of the cold she must have dozed, her fitful sleep fraught with dreams of the fleeing MacDonalds. She woke to the realisation that she was not alone. Something was moving on the periphery of her vision. The last flicker of her torch beam picked up the figure of a man approaching silently across the deer grass. Fear heightened her voice as she called out, "Who's there?"

A soft, Highland accent answered her, "Are you lost?"

"Well, yes and no", she stammered, going on to explain her predicament.

"I know the road you seek. It's too cold for you to stay here so now you must follow me."

The calm voice did not seem threatening but she prevaricated. Who was he? Where had he come from? Could she trust him?

"It's too dark for me to walk. My torch has given out. Who are you, and what are you doing on the hill on a night like this?"

"My name is MacIain and I am always on the hill this night."

What did he mean by that? Her brain felt like cotton wool and she was too tired to work it out. It felt as if the cold had penetrated the very core of her being. Her boots had leaked and she could no longer feel her feet.

"I can't see the path. I can't walk till it's lighter."

"Here - you can hold one end of this to guide you and we'll go slowly, but now you must move."

This peremptory command was accompanied by the sound of ripping material. Further dissent seemed pointless, even churlish, so she gathered herself together and off they set into the blackness with her stumbling behind holding the end of what felt like a piece of tweed. His surefooted, steady pace amazed her. 'He must have the eyes of a cat', she thought. Intermittent light from a scurrying moon was her only help. The rocks were now slippy with ice and the grass crunched beneath her boots. Watchful stags could be heard moving up the slopes as they approached and the eerie bark of a vixen seeking a mate pierced the night. *'She'll have cubs to feed at lambing time'*, she thought. Or did she say it out loud? She no longer knew. From time to time he stopped to let her rest for a few minutes but wouldn't let her sit down. She felt completely disorientated. Increasingly exhausted she lost all sense of time and the trek seemed interminable. On they went through heather, bogs and burns coming at last to a narrow isthmus where water glimmered faintly on each side.

"The twin lochans," she exclaimed, "I know where we are. This is where the hill road starts. Look, you can just see the beginnings of the path."

As they came round the shoulder of the hill, the tall man paused and stood listening. "Your people are coming for you. You'll be all right now."

Then she heard it too, the long whistle and the faint shouts and she thought she could see moving torches on the track far below.

"My whistle! Which pocket did I put it in?" She searched her anorak frantically. Her three short blasts were answered immediately by one long one. It was only as relief surged through her that she realised how scared she had been. She turned, stretching out her hand to shake that of her saviour but he was already making his way back up the hill. She watched as he climbed, to be silhouetted eventually against the lightening sky. He raised his hand in farewell before dropping down out of sight just as the rescue team reached her.

"Did you see him?" she asked, once they had checked her over and ensured that she could walk under her own steam. "He turned on the skyline just as you got here – a tall man with longish hair . . . ." Her voice tailed off as the team exchanged anxious glances.

"You've been on the hill all night and you're very cold. Let's get you down now and then you can tell us all about it." They didn't believe her. Probably thought she was hallucinating due to hypothermia. No doubt they already thought she was an idiot to land herself in this situation. Not wanting to reinforce this opinion she said nothing more.

The Landrover offered the bliss of a fleecy blanket and a mug of hot tea. Her family had been informed of her safe retrieval and she felt her spirits reviving as exhaustion took over and her eyes began to close. The rescue team had made no further reference to her tale of a guiding stranger and neither did she, but under the blanket she still held onto what looked in the interior light to be a strip of dull-coloured plaid, well-worn and frayed at the edges.

Hedgehog Highway

Irena Chapman

She snuffled through the few dry leaves around her, her sensitive nose exploring the soil beneath, ears listening for tell-tale signs of supper, her senses always alert for either food or danger. It had been a stressful day; her usual safe haven was safe no more. The large creatures she was normally aware of only occasionally and at a distance had suddenly appeared and cleared the part of her world she thought of as home; the heap of small branches, with its familiar smell and secret nest of tangled twigs and dry leaves beneath, had gone. She had fled as soon as she was startled from her tightly curled sleep, scurrying, petrified, to a dark corner behind the large black tub that smelled of old ash. Had she been seen? She had curled up for safety, trembling, with nowhere to go.

When she ventured out that evening a wasteland greeted her; not just the old wood hiding her nest but the lush mix of foxglove and dandelion, thistle, clover and daisy had gone; bare earth was neatly levelled with rounded stones piled to one side and a long black, strangely smelling cylinder of material was partly rolled out, covering most of the soil. It was tempting to explore the newly turned earth which was still exposed – but there was no protective cover for her now and she would have been far too vulnerable.

Unsettled, she set off in the direction of her usual night's foraging; and also one of her little bolt holes that she had made just off her path, somewhere to hide in case of danger or a sudden downpour. The wildlife of this part of the world is well aware we can have four seasons in a day! But - there was a problem. There was something in the way. It was wood, delightfully smelling freshly cut wood (sadly too fresh for any bugs to have made a home) – but it shouldn't be there! And there was so much of it! So many upright flat pieces lined up next to each other. She made short runs up and down alongside it, turning and going back and back again as though if she did this enough times she would somehow find a way through, but there was none. Stopping briefly she sniffed the air, then set off, trotting along the edge of the strange barrier, every now and again halting and standing up on her hind legs, her front paws resting against it, looking up to see if there was any way over, not understanding how it could go on for so long or be so high; she had come across fallen trees before, but this was definitely different.

She was usually an energetic wee thing and would happily cover as much as two kilometres in one night – but she was tired, her disturbed sleep and the tiny lives growing inside her were sapping her strength. She didn't often meet other hedgehogs on her travels, in fact decreasingly so, it didn't worry her at all as she, like all her species, tolerated neighbours but preferred a solitary life. There hadn't even been so many annoying males around harassing her in the spring as usual, she had only had to scare off a few before selecting her mate. However, notwithstanding how tired she was, she resolutely trotted on until eventually the ground changed, and under her delicate little feet she felt a hard knobbly surface she had experienced before, but didn't like; she usually tried to avoid it as it was home to large scary fast things with big eyes that shone in the dark. Cautiously she slowed her pace and, keeping as close to the wooden barrier as she could, she ventured forward.

Suddenly she froze, ready to curl up to protect herself, as the sound of a dog's bark cut through the quiet night. She waited, fearful, testing the air for any sounds or smells of an approaching animal, feeling exposed with nothing but the plain wood of the barrier beside her, but not daring to move. The barking stopped and after a while she felt a little calmer, the only sounds the gentle rustle of leaves in the evening breeze; sensing it was safe to continue she carefully moved forward.

At last! The barrier had ended! She peeked around the edge, then, relieved to see her way was clear, quickly skirted round it and set off to head back down the other side as fast as she could.

Finally, finally, she was in a better space, plants and soil bounded the other side of the barrier and increasingly familiar smells reassured her, as she sensed she was nearing her own range she relaxed and slowed her pace. Feeling confident and more secure she could at last seek her supper; turning away from the new wood she foraged her way along her familiar route, picking up the tiny hints of her prey moving amongst the dead leaves and just beneath the soil. She was reassured to recognise the aromatic scent of the bramble bush that hid her bolt hole as she neared it, a quick inspection confirmed it was still intact, secreted under a dense mass of stems, safe and dry. Assured she had this to come back to she continued on. A considerable number of slugs, bugs and earthworms had been consumed by the time she had traversed across the end of the back garden she was now in when another shock met her – another barrier, just like the first! It smelt the same, felt the same, and again as she explored up and down along it, gave her no way through.

Exhausted and confused she stopped, the stressful day and tiring night were really taking their toll now and the light of dawn was already hinting at its presence in the sky. She abandoned her attempt to follow her usual routine and returned the way she had come, breaking her habit of not taking too much food from any one part of her foraging range she sought out more to eat on the way. She returned to her little bolt hole, it would make a good nest, it was well hidden and she now set about making it roomier and more cosy, pulling in some extra dry grass and leaves before settling to an uneasy sleep.

She awoke during the day to a loud humming sound, vibrations through the ground further unsettling her. Creeping to the front of her newly upgraded nest she cautiously looked out. Unable to see anything, she was however aware of the smell of the large creatures who were clearly somewhere close at hand. Unhappily she retreated further into her sanctuary and stayed very still, curled up in her spikey ball, until at last the sounds and vibrations ceased and sleep returned.

When evening came she woke again, cautiously sniffing the air before emerging. Instinctively she turned for her old home, retracing her way along her familiar route. The barrier was still there but it was different; as she investigated she found that a gap, a nice hedgehog sized gap, had appeared at the bottom since the previous evening. She carefully looked through. Unfortunately, that was where the good news ended. Her old home was now an expanse of the oddly uniform rounded stones, tall things made of curiously coloured dead wood sat on the stones, and sticks which shone a harsh light from their tops chased away any safe shadows. She shuddered and turned back, making her way past the hidden entrance to her new home, continuing along her old route towards the second barrier. She was well rested and ready to meet it and whatever challenges it brought.

What she found there was an even better surprise – a new hole had appeared in this barrier too! Cautiously she crept through, all the while alert for danger. It was safe. As she trotted on the smell of the new wood soon faded, replaced by the familiar scents and landmarks of her foraging path and, happily confident she could come and go safely to her new nest, she eagerly set off for a good night's hunting.

Flotsam along the Underpath

Alex Breck

My tears had dried as the two of us sat in the warmth of the autumn afternoon and my bitter words began tumbling out, unstoppable now after fermenting for twenty-five years. The man had been a complete stranger to me until a few moments earlier when he had found me crying quietly to myself. Still shaking from my earlier encounter along the beach, I had subjected him to the whole sorry story...

"You drink so much of that stuff love, maybe you *should* start that vineyard you're always going on about!"

I'd been joking when I'd said that to Jamie after we'd spent yet another sozzled weekend. The exact words he used in his uncharacteristically defeatist reply would be seared across my heart for eternity. "Aye, maybe, but I wouldn't have a ghost of a chance raising that kind of cash, these days, would I?"

Poor Jamie had invested his pile into a chain of ski-shops just as the warmest spell of winters for a generation dealt the industry a death blow from which it would never recover. Financially and spiritually bankrupted by the business collapse, we had just escaped to the Argyll Coast for a cheap week away from the constant reminders of our failure. It was either that or a short walk off the Kessock bridge.

I would often think back to the moment he waved me off that day, clearly relishing an unaccompanied stroll around the many quirky shops of the sea-side town. Instead, Bonnie and I headed for the windy beach and a hard, restorative walk along the underpath. We were still youngish and reasonably fit back then, both our boys were away at college and despite our recent catastrophe, I was proud of my strong and beautiful Jamie. I can still remember thinking how much I longed to make everything right again for us. Never had the sun felt so deliciously warm to me that day, glinting in his mischievous eyes, his still-thick red hair shining brightly as he turned away and strode off into the busy throng.

Within a short time, we'd already walked a long way out from the town. The dog had disappeared amongst the wild bushes, chasing her imaginary rabbits and I was innocently rooting around looking for interesting pieces of driftwood to take back for Jamie. A particularly attractive log, shaped like a silvered dolphin, was pinning down a gorgeous old leather bag. Being of a nosy disposition, I thought I would take a quick look inside it as I weighed up my chances of fitting the piece of driftwood into the back of the estate. Although a little worn and battered, the bag had obviously once been a fine object and I decided it was perhaps the quality of small leather case that a country doctor would have carried on his rounds.

My heart began beating uncontrollably in my neck as I prised open the bag to see a large amount of bank notes, neatly bundled. I stood up immediately and looked surreptitiously around me and high up towards the rocky cliff behind, already feeling as if I had broken the rules. There were black spots whizzing across my eyes and I thought I was going to pass out. But there wasn't a soul anywhere in sight and so I dropped back down to my haunches, my face now cauldron-hot as I guiltily opened the stiff leather a little wider than before. There was no doubt! It was a substantial amount of cash and I guessed there had to be several thousand at least.

Without a moment's thought, I snapped the bag shut and wrestled it out of the sand. My head spinning, I began walking along the narrowing path as fast as I dared, heading away from the town and out towards the headland. I couldn't believe what I was doing! I needed some time to think. Looking over my shoulder as I walked, trying frantically to whistle for the dog but failing due my extreme agitation, I called her, my voice sounding high-pitched and foreign. Feeling slightly comforted by her re-appearance, I continued to walk on, yet all the time expecting the siren of a police car or a heavy hand on my shoulder.

Much later, I made my way back to town and headed straight for the hotel hoping that Jamie would have returned by now. With my head down and rehearsing madly as I walked, I was oblivious to the cacophony of noise echoing off the old buildings of the town centre. The ambulances and fire-engines rushing past could never compete with the fireworks going off inside my head.

Looking back now, as I often do, I want to be sick, as I remember how I was almost kissing the seductive heap of money piled on top of our hotel bed. Several hours had passed and I hadn't even considered why Jamie hadn't returned to the room. It was only when I felt the light changing as the late afternoon sun dropped behind taller buildings opposite, that I suddenly looked at my watch.

I was so excited, I couldn't wait a second longer and so after clumsily wrapping the hotel bedspread over the loot, I headed down to the hotel lobby to try and find him. Downstairs, the cramped hotel doorway was darkened by several large men in black and I stopped dead in my tracks wondering how on earth I would ever be able to explain my stupidity to Jamie and the boys. To this day, I could kick myself for my selfishness, as it never crossed my mind that something may have happened to him.

It had been a hit-and-run, they said. Killed outright, he would never have known a thing. The driver had been blind drunk, a local man, now in custody.

The distance of time hadn't diminished my grief and I took a break from my story to search my coat for a dry hankie. I could see the kind man nodding absentmindedly, as if my pathetic tale made any sense at all. Encouraged, but still sobbing, I continued...

The next few months had been a haze. During my heavily tranquilized mourning, I had somehow managed to drive through the rain to Edinburgh and deposit the cash in a high interest account where it was almost forgotten about for a year or so.

There had been a great deal more money than I had first realised that terrible day, far out along the windswept coastal pathway. Several hundred thousand more. The interest accrued over the first year alone was more than the paltry salary from my dull office job. Sitting in solitude every evening, I had plenty time to think and so after yet another sleepless night, instead of turning right for the employee car-park the next morning, I drove straight past. I didn't stop. I didn't even slow down, all the way through the early morning darkness, headed East, until I arrived at the bank. Then, feeling like a gangster, I withdrew a large chunk of cash and filled the old car with the reckless beginnings of a vineyard collection.

My life seemed destined to travel a new path. I relocated to a lush area near Ullapool, warmed by the waters of the Gulf Stream, and read and re-read all Jamie's careful plans about the wine business. With my 'Beach Investment' underpinning the venture, I could afford to be brave and innovative and so within two years my vines were flourishing and now, over twenty years later, the boys and I have a successful vineyard, micro-brewery, online export business and tourist centre.

So, I explained tearfully. "That's what's brought me back here, to the scene of the crime. I was on the way to a Scottish wine growing conference in Oban."

"And then you met our old Davy! He's been plaguing this stretch of the beach for years..."

I had only just explained my frightening experience moments before which had prompted his timely kindliness in sitting with me, to hear my confession. But neither of us had been prepared for the revelations that were to result from this chance meeting.

Apparently, I had not been the first wandering tourist to be accosted by the elusive, wild-eyed tramp who inhabited the bushes along the coastal pathways. Hair matted with dirt and a leather-skinned face lacerated by years of rough sleeping, 'old Davy' had been able to evade the authorities with ease and after a while they'd just resigned themselves to giving out a vague warning not to walk too far along the beach underpath alone.

My encounter had been a shocking experience. Pointing at me and literally jumping up and down with a fevered excitement, he had hissed the same words repeatedly. I wouldn't have described him as being overly aggressive. Instead it was more his alarming demeanour and the piercing intensity of his dark eyes that had transfixed me so. Crazily, I remembered thinking somehow, he seemed almost pleased to see me as he whispered his strange message.

"We paid the price…, didn't we?

You and me. We paid dear, we did.

You couldn't leave things be, your perfect crime…

We paid dear…"

It was only then that my Good Samaritan explained to me that, thanks to my story, he now knew, for the very first time, who the real 'old Davy' actually was.

'Old Davy', he had said, without any fanfare, must have been a local low-life, Will Higgins, who had taken a significant step up the criminal ladder when he had been given the important job of hiding the proceeds from a local bank job for just one day. But the money had quickly gone missing and so shortly afterwards, no doubt consumed with fear, along with the best part of a bottle of rum, he had ploughed into a tourist on a zebra crossing.

Upon realising the significance these words would have for me, Charles, my new confidant, had remained silent for a long time, allowing me the chance to get it all off my chest.

I'd never known what had caused the accident and I'd taken no interest in the outcome of the trial beyond the small comfort in knowing the driver had been jailed for a long time. Now, after so many years of hating the man who had taken away my beloved Jamie, then meeting him face-to-face in such a confrontational manner, I had been surprised to feel only pity for the deranged old man.

Because I had chosen to wander that beach path all those years ago, I had been complicit in the death of my husband, yet it was Higgins who had been sent to prison for half a lifetime. By the look of him just then, he'd obviously suffered greatly, while I, although grief-stricken for the loss of my husband, had moved on with my life to profit considerably from my beachcombing haul. I remarked upon this revelation, after a considerable period of silence, the cooling early evening breeze gently reminding us that we had been sitting for too long. Charles just stared back at me, his eyes wide with apprehension.

"You really don't understand, do you...? Higgins never left prison. He was stabbed to death almost twenty years ago. It's his *ghost* that's been stalking this sandy underpath ever since!"

Charles and I have remained firm friends ever since and write often. Neither of us are remotely surprised that old Davy has never again been seen walking the wild and windy shoreline.

Horses at Dusk, Glen Lonan. Photograph by Leonie Charlton

Pony Paths

Leonie Charlton

Author's note. English translations have been substituted for Gaelic place names to safeguard the location of golden eagle nest sites.

It's late August and I've been walking the pony paths in this glen with you since early June. Now the frogs are half-grown, no longer springing like tiddlywinks from under our feet. Gold rush of bog asphodel is over, empty flower shells relaxing to rust. Meanwhile the Scotch argus butterflies have exploded, we're passing through dark sweet clouds of them now. It's been fifteen years since ponies took deer off the hills here, and today there are no Highland garrons living in the glen; Lintel, Morag and Duke, Amber and Jodie, all long-buried. Yet the paths cleave on, works of craft and hard graft and rock. Works of art.

I walk with the stick you gave me. The shank is hazel cut locally. The handle is carved from the horn of a tup you found on the hill - he'd fallen into a hole and died there. Twenty odd years ago you'd shot his horns off, a stick maker couldn't leave them to go to waste, you'd told me. I imagined the pink scud of the exposed quick. I shuddered, it sounded violent. Hard to sync that to the soothing heft of horn now fitting my palm. The lucent aliveness of it, how it catches every colour and mood of the day. This is a careworn stick, you'd taken it to the hill yourself for years, replaced its shank many times, before giving it to me.

You and this stick know the pony paths so well. I walk them with you both. I feel very lucky. Today we are high on The Rough Hill. It is early August and hot. Sweat pours down my back and we drink at a pool where Morag used to drink on her way to collect deer shot on The Round Top of the Birches. We're keeping well above The Burn of Split Stones. You hold a lot of store by not losing height, it saves energy and time. The water below breathes over a perfection of madder-rose rock, my lungs want to float me down there, let my toes trail through the uppermost needles of the Scots pines on the way. These trees that have survived against centuries' of odds. Previous owners loved the pine trees, got helicopters in and fenced the area off to protect them from grazing. The pine trees were infertile through old age so seedlings were brought in from outside. The old and new are flourishing. Long-standing pines must know everything there is to know of this place, mapping it all in the jigsaw of their bark: each birth, love and bare-boned death; every secret of wolf, vole and cone; every land-use change, displacement and replacement; summering of cattle, gathering of sheep, then the last cow walked out of here, last of the lambs sold. And when the hydroelectric power schemes go in next year, and the pines' roots are shaken by heavy machinery, they will feel yet one more tremble of time.

In this stronghold of golden eagles, this curved place where voices of land and water and sky can be heard crystalline clear, you urge me to think positively. This glen has seen so much action over the millennia, at the hand of ice and human, it can surely cope. And maybe the current owners will put money generated from the hydro schemes back into this generous place; into restoration and regeneration projects, like the one in the remnant pine forest below; perhaps even the repopulation of this glen, now there is only you, one man living here, an all-time low. I follow you through a gate that after fifty years is still hung to within a millimetre of perfection. You point out the workmanship, how every fencepost is straight, every wire still taught. You shake your head in admiration. Simple things, in the here and now, that make sense to you - that are full of meaning and connect you to the people who have worked here before you.

These pony paths are the same, painstakingly built, often over older pre-existing paths, by people who knew what they were doing, who built things to last. We're following the cairns - large glacially deposited rocks with small stones placed on top by stalkers and ghillies - that mark the pony path. It is a slow hot dance, my heart is pounding into the hush of the hillside. From here, on the other side of the glen, two more pony paths are visible following burns that curve round each side of The Hill of the Hinds. I lift a hand to my chest, feel the paths like the lines on my own palm. I have walked them slowly with you, you who knows them by heart, and my own heart is now mapped forever by them. I feel the pony paths, all four of them, in the warm open spread of my hand. Fingers following feet, step by step, up burns and into high corries. A palm full of story and suggestion, stillness and storm. From up here I can see how the deer paths cross them, running like threads of bruise and grace through the history of it all.

The path curving round the west face of The Hill of the Hinds is the pony path I know best, I've walked it three times now. The first was with you this time last year. I was captivated by your stories, steadied by your pace. We were shadowed that day by a juvenile golden eagle and you told me how the eagles are your friends, how they know you, have been watching your every move for thirty years. They recognise the measure of your step, the bright of your hair, sense in the air the days you will leave deer gralloch for them. The second time was with my friend and our two Highland ponies, Ross and Chief. We were training Ross for the deer. You shot a hind and Ross carried her down off the hill that day. We'd loaded him on the other side of the burn among the shielings at the bottom of The Black Glen. Ross was willing, the work still present in his Rùm blood, but he was twenty and his hips were sore and we all knew he wouldn't be doing too much more of this work.

The third time on that path was this June. I passed Ross' droppings, still there on the path from last year, and I cried. I cried because he's getting older, and I won't take him on hard high hills anymore. I cried for the passing of time. There will be other ponies you'd said, I just need to cry for this one, I'd replied. It had helped to walk behind you, filling your steps with my own presence, forgetting and thinking only about where to place each foot, and counting frogs. When we got to the shielings - and the crossing place where months before Ross had ferried the hind across the burn - a dipper spun past us, sat bobbing on a rock up to its tiny knees in torrent, a miracle of resistance. As we walked higher the scoop of the corrie wavered in a heat haze. I was carried into the thinness of this place, the closeness of other worlds. Under The Round Top of the Cattle I could almost hear the molinia grass being torn by cattle mouths, high voices lifting from the shielings, taste woodsmoke and warm milk. I heard too the calls of a greenshank, so insistent that I lifted my binoculars. Eventually I saw it, but only in flight, skimming over the tussocks. When it landed it became invisible once more. The first greenshank I'd seen here. We walked on through that shimmering place, following cairns and crossing trout-plucked pools, up towards The Sandy Bealach bowing pink with broken granite, to where the watershed tips over. On the other side was The Corrie of the Twisted Ones, a hard and hungry place you said. You pointed out up on our left The Corrie of Snow, where you'd shot a stag one day, and as you dragged him out another stag had followed you. It was horrible, you said, horrible - you'd shot his friend, never seen anything like that before or since, they'd probably never been apart.

We walked back down through a spin of dragonflies. You told me that's why hobbies like it up there, they hunt the dragonflies. You used to see ring ouzels in this place. We saw neither hobbies, nor ring ouzels, nor eagles nor deer that day. It was important, you said, to tell the world that the deer numbers weren't here anymore, all this talk of too many deer, well where were they then? Being annihilated in the commercial plantations, their travel routes cut off by fences. You believe in a world where deer and trees co-exist. Deer are forest animals, after all. Aye, but it's complicated, you sigh. They're just not here, the deer, and Scotland without deer, well that thought breaks your heart. Each time we walk you talk to me of where you would plant trees if you had the say, the deer fences could be taken down after thirty years. Stands of woodland in your mind's eye, bits best suited to rowan or aspen or birch. Juniper too and Scots pine. You paint trees into the landscape for me, for the deer, you fill my ears with birdsong and the thud of resin-blackened antlers in the rut, and the roars, all the roars. But no wolves, no wolves in these trees of yours. You are most adamant. That's my dream, you say, fill your boots you say, but it wouldn't work, there just isn't the space anymore. They'd be persecuted. More pain. More trouble.

There on the east side of The Hill of the Hinds is the other pony path, the one that shadows a steep deep burn, and I can see the single-plank swing bridge you built that crosses it down near where it joins the river - a bridge that makes dogs cower and stomachs turn. My eyes home in on this second pony path, a steady green line inclining westwards to pines up above in the gully, yes, more Scots pines hanging on in a final hold; safe there from axe and fire, sheep and deer, surviving where they are forced to survive. The tree stock is strong and resilient, like the people who must have lived in these places, I think to myself, before they ran out of toe-holds.

The July day we'd walked up that second pony path on The Hill of the Hinds it was hot and close, I was struggling. You were kind, took care of me, as you do. We drank from pools, and I stopped often to admire the path, patches of plaited stonework still perfectly in place, slabs set snugly over burns like lintel stones. Lintel was the name of your favourite deer pony - you said she'd been good craic, had trusted you. You told me about the day you'd fallen asleep as ponyman, it was a Saturday, you'd likely had a hangover. The stalking party hadn't been able to rouse you, not even by lighting a fire and sending smoke signals. In the end they'd had to send the ghillie down to wake you. You laughed remembering as we followed the path to where it ended at The Spying Point. We carried on to the summit, at over 3, 000 feet it is a Munro; at the bottom the bog asphodel had been at the peak of its flowering, at The

Spying Point it was just budding, and finally there on the tops there was none.

It had been like tundra up there. Worlds of tiny lichens and plants I didn't recognise bound tight to the ground, with antlers and eyes and bright colours. You showed me a mountain hare's shelter, a small natural cave, full of droppings, and pointed out the livid moss marking a spring in the hard, high ground. Up on the very top the ravens met us, lifting off their shit-splattered rock with casual ease. We lay out of the wind and watched two walkers fool around taking selfies on the summit cairn. You said they were great, you loved how they were having so much fun. We waved at them. They were exuberant back. Some peoples' faces cloud over when they see your stick, your dog, your tweed. After the women had left the ravens found their apple cores. They swallowed and hopped as you and I shared a bag of nuts and raisins.

I'm pulled back to this butterfly-hot August day on the steep side of The Rough Hill, your hand has come behind you in an urgent 'get down' gesture. We both drop. Ahead of us, fifty yards away, two stags are leaning into the hill - knees and hips at uncanny angles, the deep velvet on their antlers holding light like rain. We two humans and the two stags watched each other for a long while; through my binoculars I could see their calm interested expressions, their periodic chewing. They stood at their leisure. They just know we're not stalking, you say, such clever beasts. Then they're gone, over the top, and my thoughts float with them down to the fourth pony path that runs up The Pass of the Storms. I think back to its steady climb of spider webs and pyramidal morraine, its Scots pine that crowns all of the others and the pony post longstanding above it. You'd told me that day how that path, its smell of dry heath, always reminded you of home on the east coast, you'd pointed to the spread of pink, wild thyme. As we'd walked through patches of lain-down-upon grass and the taut-sweet smell of deer, you told me if it was your shout you'd have planted this whole burnside with native woodland. You pointed out the old Drovers Road, at the head of the corrie it turned into a series of sharp zigzags where they used to walk the cattle up and over the top, then down into the neighbouring glen. We talked about how in the past people had trodden lightly, using only what they needed, leaving barely a trace - just this, a memory of walking, still so green from long ago dung. "We need light hands and feet, now more than ever... see there, at the foot of the zigzag path, you can bring a pony round between The Round Top Where There Are Birch Trees, and The

Hill of Wild Garlic. Then down onto The Greens to meet up with The Rough Hill pony track."

Today, on the top of The Rough Hill, surrounded by the imprint of these four pony paths, a single painted lady butterfly sashays past. We're on the lookout for a juvenile golden eagle. A week ago a landslide wiped out its nest. All that rain we've had - you've never known the ground so 'full' - has destabilised the ground. The chick was right on the point of fledging. You're hopeful that it will be safe somewhere, that its parents will be taking care of it. I am anxious. You've borrowed my ears, your own a roar of tinnitus, and I'm listening out for the insistent peep of a young eagle. It's been a bad year for golden eagles, this was the only pair to successfully breed in the area. I think the chick will be fine, you say. I wish I shared your optimism. As we eat our lunch of salted almonds and cheese the female parent bird shows herself, distinguishable by her size, her darkness, the spaces on her left wing where she's missing primary feathers. I am thrilled to see her. It's a perfect day, you say, standing up.

I look back across the glen to the top of The Hill of the Hinds, I breathe in all the space between, hoping hard that the young eagle has survived the wreckage of its nest, the premature slide into the unknown. I pick up my hazel stick, let it take my full weight, *Can you divine the future of this thin and precious place?* I ask it. We start the steep descent down towards the river, its pools glinting in golden brown. You told me there's been a good run of salmon in the river this year, and now the hazelnuts are ripening. Even as we spin towards environmental collapse, I feel a flicker of faith that wisdom can still break through. I step down over the falling away ground as swallows strike ancient knowings against a clear sky, and two damselflies, locked in mating, crackle past like newly-lit fire.

Writing 'The Path'

Bob Toynton

Ronald thought in images, in patterns, in rhythms. Sometimes these, especially while walking, brought with them words. Softly chanted inwardly, many would call these words poetry, but only much later.

In the cool of a summer's morning Ronald walked, but with little rhythm, along a broad grassy path between the bracken heading, he hoped, towards the nearby coast. Even when he had lived in Argyll he had never ventured to this corner of the county. He knew of it only through Gordon.

He was walking for charity and for himself. A few months previously the hospice which would benefit from his exertions had been as unknown to him as this path. Although his colleagues had begrudgingly sponsored him, he was both relieved and slightly hurt that no-one had been interested enough to ask his motivation. Charity fatigue he speculated. Everyone was doing this sort of thing.

The dew made the path slippery in places, and the occasional large rounded stone further thwarted any attempts at a constant stride. No words were coming, but that was no surprise since Ronald was thinking of lavender.

Herbes de Provence in the American style with just enough lavender to give depth but not to be tasted. Added, with a pinch of sea-salt, to sweet white wine in which the chicken breasts are poached. Served simply with crispy roast potatoes and broccoli just softened. Balance is everything. This had been Gordon's favourite meal.

He stopped. Too much thinking was making him careless about where he placed his feet. Turning around he saw his bright green footprints on the dew-dusted grass, some wider than others where he had slid thoughtlessly and almost imperceptibly. *I must be the first along here today*, he thought as he noticed someone far behind him. Company was not what he wanted, not what he needed, and so he turned again and moved on.

Long ago Ronald had been seconded for a year to the small Argyll town where, within the first week, he met Gordon. Well, saw at least, and spoke to, but only tentatively. Four decades back for a man to show interest in another man was dangerous in so many ways. For a few weeks there had been anxiety, and that at least brought words. The walks home from the bar had been rapid and purposeful. A time to look for the courage to speak out.

> *"Orion, curse you, growing dim*
> *When I need your courage most*
> *adrift and drunk upon the rim*
> *Of sanity without the ghost*
> *ta dah ta dah ta dah ta dah…"*

Each evening the ending differed, but it would always be tense, fraught or even frightening. This, since his later work brought Ronald fame, is now the start of a well-known poem.

Back then he had walked at a rapid, even pace. That rhythm had long gone. It was odd, he thought, how when things in life were more difficult, walking seemed simpler. Now his life seemed like a straight level road, but he had lost his stride.

He delved further into this conceit. *Maybe I walked with more confidence even though the path was uneven. I'd stumble. Fine. But then I really fell. Was I winded or did I break my metaphorical bloody ankle? That's why I take more care now; walk less surely. Why the rhythm has gone, and the words.*

It was when he saw the tree that déjà vu possessed him. The broken boughs hung with lichen. The roots buckling and breaking the path ahead. The rounded cobbles like small grey whales breaching, their backs both polished and striated by centuries of rising into this well-used path. He knew that once past these obstacles and round the next corner a view to the sea would open up. A shiver went through him. He dreaded being right. Déjà vu had plagued him before and he repeated his prescription for breaking the spell. He swore loudly using words he would otherwise never use, but it felt as if they were also part of the past. He deliberately took an illogical step sideways, almost off the path. No-one would do this unless trapped in déjà vu. And then he slipped.

Meeting Gordon hadn't been a slip. It was Gordon who finally started the conversation which led to their relationship. Ronald, in his own particular way, had always pictured the small-town locals as individual strands in the pile of an exotic carpet. They clustered and made patterns on the upper side where everyone could see, but on the reverse the interweaving and knotting was indecipherable. Bloodlines and grudges, shared histories and secrets. He would always be just a stray piece of thread dropped onto the surface. Gordon was woven in tight, and so his homosexuality was, and had to remain, secret. Knowing would not cause the rug to unravel, but such a thread as Gordon, on its own, would soon fray and break.

The woman leaning over Ronald was bemused. "Folk often curse as they fall. You cursed, stepped sideways and then fell."

"I'm fine," Ronald replied. "A twist of the ankle and bruised pride. I think there's a seat round the next corner."

Later Ronald would try to describe the woman. While her face suggested great age, this was contradicted by her sureness of movement and strength as she helped him to his feet. She was small, but not petite. That was too flimsy a word. He couldn't shake from his thoughts the word *concise*. Nothing about her was superfluous.

"The path back there can be deadly," she said as they slowly rounded the corner.

"I was lost in my thoughts," Ronald replied.

"Thinking about an old friend?" she asked.

"Yes, and trying to write something in my head. The words had just started to come. Must get them down."

"Be my guest," came the reply as the woman sat in the middle of the pristine seat. "I love this place. Best view in the county," she continued.

Ronald felt he could have been offered more space, but he sat down carefully and proceeded to rummage through his rucksack. The result was a notebook and pen. He started writing

"By feet, by hooves, by scratched and polished stone,
Slow-born of memory, habit or simple will"

But as he continued, a voice started to recite, at first just a moment behind his writing.

"It threads through stories of those who are long gone."

Disconcerted, but not wishing to disrupt the flow, he continued with the next line.

"Who walked, who looked, who stumbled on these hills".

By the time he got to 'stumbled' the voice had overtaken his writing.

Even before his pen stopped moving he looked up, prepared to be angry at this invasion of his privacy and his space. The woman sat perfectly still; her head erect and eyes tight closed.

"That's good," she said, "not just the words but the way they have the faltering rhythm which only comes with time; with age."

"How did you do that?"

"Know what you were going to write?" she confirmed.

"Yes. I'd only that moment found the words."

"The essence, the spirit of this place. But how are you feeling now?" she asked, changing the topic rather clumsily. "Your friend. Shall I call him?"

"Him? Why do you assume it's *him*?"

"How did you know this seat was here?" she responded.

"I must have been here before. I feel I have been."

"This seat was only put here yesterday. Did your friend tell you?"

"He died a few years ago," Ronald replied.

"Was it your fault?"

"No!"

"Then why do you feel so guilty?" she asked, and Ronald realised he was now in her gaze.

"I let him down."

"He told you that?" she asked.

"No. I'd not seen him for years. But I could have helped him. He might have listened to me,"

Ronald said softly. "But how did you know those words? What I was about to write?" he continued, regaining his composure.

"Do you sometimes feel you know somewhere, even though you've never been there before?"

"That's what I was feeling when you saw me fall. Déjà vu. Strong déjà vu. I get it quite often."

"Just means 'already seen'" she replied.

"But I hadn't seen. I haven't been here before."

"But you sense you've been here. Is that not memory?"

"No. This place is new to me, but it doesn't feel like it."

"When you sense something is wrong, which sense are you using?"

Hearing this question Ronald realised this was not someone prepared to just pass the time of day.

"None. It's just a feeling. Well, not touch-feeling, just a thought, an emotional feeling."

"So, not physical. Some feelings, some senses pass straight into your mind. No ears, eyes or fingers involved. A straight pathway, slipping straight past the other senses. Do you dream?" she continued.

"Yes of course. Sometimes."

"And you?" Ronald asked.

"When I did," she replied, "I'd always wonder which was the memory: the dream or the remembering of the dream. Can you know something you can't remember, and if something triggers your memory, even years later, how do you distinguish the knowing from the dreaming?"

"So how did you know what I was about to write?"

"I sensed it, the same way you knew this seat was here. Your friend, did he know this place?"

"He always wanted to bring me here. It just never happened."

"How did he die?" she asked rather bluntly.

"On his own. Well in a hospice. His family might have been there. I don't know."

"Of what?"

"Cancer, apparently, on the Death Certificate. A rare one. But AIDS let it kill him."

"Did you...?"

"No," Ronald said with relief, "it's nearly forty years since we were together. We kept in touch. Just a phone call, or maybe two, each year. He'd tell me what he'd been up to and I'd read him what I'd managed to write."

"He never forgot you," Ronald heard the woman say softly, but he wasn't sure whether it was a question or just her thinking aloud.

"We'd been very close for a year or so, but he couldn't leave this part of the world behind. When he tried, I could see he was unhappy, so we parted. Good friends. Always good friends."

"Sad", and as she said the word, Ronald felt it within himself but also in her.

"A couple of years ago he called and asked if I would visit and cook his favourite meal. Out of the blue, after all those years. I never asked why."

"You don't just miss a person, but all that goes with them," she spoke softly.

"I knew I had to go abroad for a while so I put him off and told him I'd be back in touch as soon as I returned. But things were hectic. The more time passed the more difficult it became. About four months later I finally phoned. The number was dead."

"But that could have been for any number of reasons," she responded. Ronald noticed tears starting to form in her eyes, mirroring his own.

"That's when I realized that he'd been trying to tell me something. In the previous couple of calls he'd said things. I felt so stupid. It all fell into place. None of his family or friends up here even suspected he was gay. No-one to talk to. No-one to push him to get help."

Ronald felt the woman's hand on his. "He was an adult. It was his decision. His secret to keep or not."

"I know," said Ronald, "but if I'd realised earlier, if I'd gone and cooked his damned meal, I could have pushed him to get help. He might still be here."

"He preferred to die with his secret intact than live with the whispers, glances and pity of a community that meant everything to him," she whispered softly.

"No... I don't know" Ronald hesitated.

The woman's hand squeezed Ronald's just for a moment and, as if sharing a treasured secret of her own, she said in a voice as warm as her hand was cold, "You misunderstand. I wasn't asking a question." Then letting go his hand and rising to her feet she continued, "I shouldn't really be here. I just came to try out this new seat. You should be fine now. The path's more even from here on and the dew's starting to burn off. Anyway, time to make tracks."

An image came into Ronald's mind and he couldn't help but exclaim, "That's the next line of the poem!"

"On this track, which I renew beneath my heels"

"Good. It's got the same uneven gait," she replied.

"And then," added Ronald,

"Dusted sage by fragile early morning dew
The grass is polished emerald with each tread"

"Just one line will finish it," the woman said, "but I must go."

"No. Wait. Help me with the last bit. Gordon was my muse. I lost him!" Ronald exclaimed.

"Talk to him," came the reply.

"But he's dead!"

Seeing the confusion in his face, the woman sat down again.

"People talk to the dead all the time. Best not to do it out loud. Not in public at least. But it's nice to have a chat. Just don't expect to hear the reply through your ears every time. Gordon was right. You can be slow on the uptake." And with that she smiled, stood up again and started to walk away.

It was only as Ronald lifted his rucksack onto the seat ready to pack away his notebook that he first saw the small plaque screwed to the backrest.

'*Mary Robertson. She loved this old path and this place.*'

With that the final line came into Ronald's head

"*Reminding me, however old the path, each step is new*".

He scribbled it down, then read out the whole poem to himself.

"*By feet, by hooves, by scratched and polished stone*
Slow-born of memory, habit or simple will
It threads through stories of those who are long gone
Who walked, who looked, who stumbled on these hills.

On this track, which I renew beneath my heels
Dusted sage by fragile early morning dew
The grass is polished emerald with each tread
Reminding me, however old the path, each step is new."

And then he realised.

"Mary," he shouted after the figure disappearing into the distance, "thanks."

He was almost sure he saw her turn for a moment, just before she disappeared, her arm raised in acknowledgement. But Ronald was distracted by an old familiar voice. "That's good. Now send it off somewhere and get it published."

Homeward Bound. Photograph by Julie Dawson

Other publications by the writers featured here

Short Stories

2018 "Sea Passages" Seilachan Fort (Ed. Alex Breck, & including many of the writers here)

2016 "The Changeling" in "Secrets and Confessions" Scottish Book Trust (Alison Dawson)

2016 "Your Call or Mine" in "Secrets and Confessions" Scottish Book Trust (Jeni Rankin)

2014 "Coming Home" in "Stories from Home" Scottish Book Trust (Sylvia Smith)

Travel Memoirs / New Nature Writing

2020 "Marram" Sandstone Press Ltd.

(Leonie Charlton)

Poetry

2018 "Birds the Colours and Shapes of Leaves" Hammerinn Books (Bob Toynton)

Thrillers by Alex Breck

2017 "The Piper's Promise" Seilachan Fort

2016 "The Devil You Know" Seilachan Fort

2016 "The Piper's Lament" Seilachan Fort

2012 "He Who Pays the Piper" Seilachan Fort